DIVINE
COMEDIES

DIVINE COMEDIES

A Gift from Zeus

and

The Old Testament Made Easy

Jeanne Steig

pictures by William Steig

A Caitlyn Dlouhy Book

Atheneum Books for Young Readers

New York London Toronto Sydney New Delhi

ATHENEUM BOOKS FOR YOUNG READERS

An imprint of Simon & Schuster Children's Publishing Division

1230 Avenue of the Americas, New York, New York 10020

For information about special discounts for bulk purchases, please contact Simon & Schuster Special Sales at 1-866-506-1949 or business@simonandschuster.com.

The Simon & Schuster Speakers Bureau can bring authors to your live event. For more information or to book an event, contact the Simon & Schuster Speakers Bureau at 1-866-248-3049 or visit our website at www.simonspeakers.com.

Book design by Ann Bobco

The text of this book is set in Adobe Caslon Pro.

The illustrations are rendered in pen and watercolor.

Manufactured in China   1115 SCP

This Atheneum Books for Young Readers edition February 2016

2 4 6 8 10 9 7 5 3 1

Library of Congress Cataloging-in-Publication Data

Steig, Jeanne.

[Works. Selections]

Divine comedies : The Old Testament made easy and A gift from Zeus / Jeanne Steig ; pictures by William Steig.

pages cm

1. Bible. Old Testament—History of Biblical events—Juvenile poetry. 2. Children's poetry, American. 3. Humorous poetry, American. 4. Mythology, Greek—Juvenile literature. I. Steig, William, 1907-2003, illustrator. II. Steig, Jeanne. Old Testament made easy. III. Steig, Jeanne. Gift from Zeus. IV. Title. V. Title: Old Testament made easy. VI. Title: Gift from Zeus.

PS3569.T344A6 2016   811'.54—dc23   2015016406

ISBN 978-1-4814-3957-2 (hardcover)

ISBN 978-1-4814-4056-1 (eBook)

CONTENTS

A Gift from Zeus

Sixteen Favorite Myths

For three goddesses:
Donna, Jane, and Suzanne

CONTENTS

PROMETHEUS

It's impossibly boring down here," said Zeus. "How on earth can you bear it?"

"Boring?" said Prometheus, one of the Titans, giants who were then Earth's only inhabitants. "White cliffs, blue seas, purple grapes, owls hooting in olive trees, everything in working order—what more could we ask for?"

"Comedy," said Zeus. "Tragedy. Let's liven it up! It's time to create men. Do something about that, will you?"

"What sort of thing are they?" asked Prometheus.

"Rather like us, but less so," replied Zeus thoughtfully. "You don't want to make their arms too long, or their legs, either. Absolutely no wings. We can't have them bumbling into Olympus, can we?"

"I'll make a stab at it," said Prometheus. He scooped up

some mud and, with a bit of help from his brother, Epimetheus, modeled a small population of men.

"They'll do," said Zeus.

"I like them," said Prometheus.

The new race of men wanted to be on good terms with the gods, so they consulted with the wily Prometheus. "We thought we'd offer up a sacrificial bull," they said. "Should we give them the meat or the bones?"

"I guess we'll let the gods decide," said Prometheus. He dismembered the bull and sewed two large bags from its hide. In one he put the meat, in the other the bones. He covered the second sack with a tempting layer of white fat and invited Zeus to choose.

"I'll take the second one," said Zeus, hungrily.

"Help yourself," answered Prometheus.

When Zeus saw how he had been tricked, he was furious; but the bones remained the share of the gods forever after.

Zeus knew who to thank for them. Prometheus would not go unpunished. "You've done these men no favor," he roared.

"These puny creatures of yours must gnaw
On meat that is stringy and tough and raw.
For the pleasure of disrespecting Zeus,
They shall not have fire. Let them eat raw goose."

"We'll see about that," said Prometheus to himself, and he went off to find the goddess Athene. "Those creatures are so helpless," he said. "They will never survive without fire."

"They *are* pathetic," sighed Athene. "But what's to be done?"

"Just sneak me into Olympus," said Prometheus. "I'll take care of the rest."

So that evening Athene smuggled him up the back side of the mountain and pointed him toward Apollo's fiery chariot. Prometheus quickly lighted a torch and flew back down to Earth, where he gave the fire to men, along with a lesson on how to use it.

> "Behold, this dancing fire I bring.
> Flame, that seems a living thing.
> Warmth, it breathes, and light—and juice
> From a freshly roasted goose!"

When Zeus saw all those twinkling fires, with succulent roasts turning above them, and men contentedly toasting their toes before them, his rage was terrible. "I'll give them a gift of my own," he shouted. "Something to make their short lives as wretched as possible!" He commissioned Hephaestus to fashion a woman—there were as yet no women—and he ordered each of the gods to endow her with a gift. Aphrodite

gave her surpassing beauty; Hermes, quickness of wit; Apollo gave her a musical voice; and the four winds gave her breath.

"What do you think?" asked Hephaestus.

"Now that's more like it," said Zeus, giving the enchanting figure an affectionate pat.

"Scrawny," said Hera, his wife, "insipid, and perhaps a bit cross-eyed." She had some misgivings about this new creation.

The woman was named Pandora, "the gift of all." "We mustn't send her off empty-handed," said Zeus. "Let's give her some baggage." So all the gods chipped in once more and put together a magnificent box packed with all the torments of mankind, which were, in that Golden Age, unknown.

"But you don't want to open it," they told her. "Not ever." Then Zeus sent her down to Earth as a present to Epimetheus.

"Think twice, brother," cautioned Prometheus. "A gift from Zeus is not likely to be a bargain." But Epimetheus was dazzled by the sight of her, and besides, he was not eager to offend Zeus by rejecting her, so he married the girl at once. They gave the mysterious box a place of honor and promised each other to leave it unopened forever.

But Pandora's lively curiosity would not let her rest. Every day she dusted it, circled it, stared at it from all angles, and tapped at it thoughtfully. One day she put her ear to it and thought she heard a faint buzzing inside. "Perhaps some poor creature is trapped in there," she said. "I'll have one little peek." And she opened it, just a crack.

What a disaster! Out flew myriad hideous things.

There were:
Carbuncles, Quagmires, and Jiggery-Pokery,
Colic, Depravity, Lummoxes, Louts,
Barbed Wire, Insomnia, Practical Jokery,
Treachery, Lechery, Deluge, and Droughts,

Truculence, Toothache, and Dandruff and Thuggery,
Blight and Sciatica, Gallstones, Tight Shoes,
Sinkholes and Nigglers, and Nits and Skullduggery,
Anchovies, Avarice, Dudgeon, The Blues.

Also:
Prissiness, Platitudes, Tapeworm, and Pestilence,
Yuckapucks, Yahoos, Delusions, and Fleas,
Heartlessness, Hiccups, Duplicity, Flatulence,
Vandals and Whiners, Ingratitude, Sleaze.

Apathy, Obloquy, Bunions, Poltroonery,
Kitsch and Cacophony, Doldrums and Pain,
Fistulas, Flimflam, Curmudgeons, Buffoonery,
Kinkiness, Stinkiness, Warts, and Chow Mein.

And more!

Pandora slammed down the lid and Epimetheus ran to help her, but it was too late. All the plagues and misfortunes that ever might be flew out of that evil box and circled twice around their heads, stinging them viciously before setting off to bedevil the life out of the human race.

At the very bottom of the box lay Hope, their only consolation. The clever Prometheus had managed to slip her in at

the last minute. Perhaps Laughter was there as well, though no one has ever bothered to mention it.

As for Prometheus, he had no hope, and nothing whatever to laugh about. Zeus would have his revenge. His henchmen, Force and Violence, seized Prometheus and brought him before the Lord of the Immortals, who drew himself up to his most godly height and thundered.

> "It seems you do not know your place.
> What are these runts, this human race,
> That you'd defy me, and conspire
> To steal my own Olympian fire?

> "Fool, hear my judgment, feel my wrath!
> Your arrogant and treacherous path
> Now plunges downward. Rest assured:
> Eternal agony is yours."

Then he ordered Force and Violence to carry Prometheus to the Caucasus, where they bound him to the mountain, in unbreakable chains. Each day an eagle came to tear out his liver, which grew back each night, so that his anguish might never cease.

After some time—between thirty and thirty thousand years—Zeus called Hermes, his messenger, and said, "Fate has decreed that one day I shall have a son. When he is grown, he will hurl me from my throne and drive all of us down into exile. Only Prometheus knows who will be the mother of this unnatural creature. Go and bargain with him; if he tells you who she is, I'll release him."

Hermes hurried to Prometheus. When he saw the Titan's agony, he was aghast. "I bring you wonderful news," he said. "Just reveal the name of the woman who will bear this child so feared by Zeus, and you'll be as free as the bird that tortures you."

But Prometheus laughed and replied, "You do indeed have wonderful news! To learn that I have such power over Zeus!

> "Every hour of pain I'll bless,
> And these chains that bind me round,
> If I'm kept a million years
> To see the tyrant, Zeus, uncrowned."

For an unfathomable time—perhaps another thirty thousand years—he went on suffering. At last the mighty Heracles, passing through the Caucasus on the way to his twelfth labor, came upon the Titan, slew the eagle, and released him from his torment.

Zeus allowed it, but he was not done with Prometheus yet. "Take a link from the chain that held you," he ordered, "and set into it a piece of the stone upon which you suffered. You must wear this circle upon your finger forever, as a sign to all the world that you are still my prisoner, and always will be." It was the first ring to be set with stone, and mankind immediately took to wearing such things themselves, as a tribute to their friend Prometheus.

Even then Zeus was not satisfied. "Wily Prometheus," he sneered, "did you actually imagine I would set you free?

"Down with you now: bleak Tartarus is your home.
No gleam of sun shall ever warm your face.

Eternal darkness shall blot out your sight,
Till some immortal begs to take your place."

So Prometheus descended to the Underworld, and certain that no immortal would ever come of his own free will to replace him there, he resigned himself to everlasting darkness.

But Heracles had not abandoned him. He remembered the centaur Chiron, whom he had once wounded accidentally. That wound would never heal, and Chiron suffered so terribly from it that he yearned for death. Unfortunately he was immortal, and could not die. So Heracles went to Chiron and said,

"Old friend, I come to pay my grievous debt:
The pain you suffer you may soon forget
In Tartarus, where Prometheus thirsts for light
As you the solace of eternal night."

Chiron eagerly agreed to exchange his immortality for Prometheus's place in Tartarus, and the Titan was finally free to return to the upper earth.

Prometheus never did reveal the woman's name, nor did he ever have the pleasure of seeing Zeus driven from Olympus. Perhaps the son who is destined to do it has yet to be born.

DEMETER

Hades, Lord of the Underworld, was on one of his rare visits to the upper earth when his eye fell upon a fair young girl, and he was instantly ablaze with love. Wishing to do things in the proper way, he went up to Olympus to call on his younger brother, Zeus. "I'm in love," declared Hades.

"A wonderful feeling," said Zeus. "Who is she? A plump little mortal? A wiggly, giggly nymph?"

"No, no," said Hades. "Your daughter, Kore. Our sister Demeter's girl. My niece. Yours, too, come to think of it. And her mother's." The Olympians were a happy-go-lucky lot, for all their jealousy and mischief, and such distinctions were of small concern. "I've come to ask for her hand—and all the rest of her!"

"Well," replied Zeus. "Now." It was a dodgy situation. Demeter would never forgive him if he agreed to banish her daughter to the eternal gloom of Tartarus. Hades would be hellishly angry if he refused. "I can't say yes; I can't say no," he murmured, with a significant lift of his majestic brow.

"Enough said," replied his understanding brother, with a smile. And he wasted no more time in Olympus.

Demeter and Kore were almost inseparable. Demeter, great goddess of the harvest, had been a frisky girl, and her daughter delighted in tales of her mother's old romances. Kore had no lover yet. Though she gossiped cheerfully about the boys who caught her eye, she preferred her mother to any of them.

The day after the conversation on Olympus, Kore was strolling in the fields with her friends. She had wandered off by herself and was just reaching for a tuft of jonquils when a terrible roaring filled the little glen, and the earth exploded. Hades, in his gleaming chariot with its night-dark steeds, burst up from the Underworld and seized Kore. On the ravaged earth he ravaged the girl, swept her into his chariot with her gown torn and her body bloodied, and carried her down, straight down to the depths of Tartarus, from which there is no returning. Her anguished cries rang through the hills and fields even as the earth closed over her head, but only Hecate, goddess of witches, darkness, and the dead, heard them. Hecate ran to find her, but no trace of Kore remained.

The other girls went to Demeter. "She was laughing with

us. Then she went off to pick flowers, and we never saw her again," they said, shaking their heads in bewilderment.

"Where is Kore?" wailed Demeter. "She would never abandon me. No, someone bewitched her, someone has drawn her away. But I will find her. If she is on this green earth, I will find my daughter!" Calling for Kore she flew, without resting, for nine days and nights, from desert to city, from gardens to desolate wastes, not overlooking the farthest islands, the deepest caverns, the iciest peaks.

Her feet bled and her voice was more of a hiss than a whisper. She would eat nothing, she would drink nothing, she refused to sleep. On the tenth day, Hecate came upon her, exhausted and despairing.

"I have not seen your daughter," said the crone, "but I have heard her calling 'Mother, oh Mother!' so pitifully. Hades has taken her. He carried her down to the Kingdom of the Dead and made her his queen."

Then the poor mother was out of her mind with rage and sorrow. She raised her fists to the heavens and called out,

"I curse the earth that witnessed her anguish:
May it be blighted, may it languish!
My curse on the land that let her be taken:
May it be bleak, and godforsaken.
Until she returns, till my arms enfold her,
Let it grow colder, colder, colder!"

And it was so. Nothing blossomed. Every living thing withered and died, the birds whose songs she had loved to hear with her daughter were silenced, and the earth was barren.

The mortals suffered. Demeter saw their misery, but she would not relent. "Zeus is behind this," she said. "Hades would never have dared to kidnap my daughter if Zeus had not given him leave." So she turned her back on Olympus, disguised herself as an ancient woman, and wandered the parched earth, lamenting for Kore. She came to Eleusis and was sitting beside a well with her fingers tangled in her hair, when four charming sisters came to fill their jugs.

"Are you ill?" they asked her. "Perhaps we can help you?"

"I have escaped with my life from pirates, who wanted to sell me as a slave, and I am, as you see me, a weary and friendless stranger," said the goddess, whose wits were wandering.

"How awful," they said. "Just sit quietly here, while we run back with our jugs and ask our parents, King Celeus and Queen Metaneira, if they will take you in."

The girls ran off and soon returned to lead her to their house, where Metaneira embraced her and gave her sweet mint-flavored barley water to drink. Just then Abas, King Celeus's son, came in, and saw how thirstily Demeter was drinking. "Old woman, you swill like a pig!" he jeered. Demeter, enraged, threw her drink straight into his face, whereupon he shrank down into a minuscule spotted newt and slithered squealing away under the door.

"I'm sorry," sighed Demeter to his shocked parents. She took the newborn son from Metaneira's arms and held him tenderly. "Please let me be nursemaid to little Demophoön, to atone for my carelessness," she begged. She thought she would make up to the unhappy parents for the loss of their older son by giving the infant eternal life. To this end, each night after the mortals had gone to bed, she placed Demophoön in the middle of the fire, saying,

"The thread of thy life shall not be severed.
Grow, and flourish, and live forever."

All went well, and the baby did flourish; but one night Metaneira came back to the room and, seeing her child in the flames, she screamed. Again Demeter lost her temper, snatched him up, and flung him to the ground. The spell was broken, and the baby died.

Then Demeter threw off her old woman's cloak and wrinkles and declared herself: "I am the goddess Demeter! I, too, have lost my dearest child. My arms are empty. My wrath is terrible, and my grief is inconsolable. You must build me a temple in Eleusis. There I will make my home, there I will grieve, and there you must worship me." Metaneira and her daughters shrank back in terror; they vowed to the goddess that they would do as she required. The next day they called together the villagers, and work on the great temple was begun.

Demeter continued her wandering. She was seen in every part of the world, raving, cursing the earth and making it die. When the temple at Eleusis was finished, she returned to it, and sat, silent, unmoving. Her shivering, famished worshipers

implored her to restore the earth to life, but it remained as cold as the goddess, and as barren.

Zeus, realizing that all life on earth was doomed to extinction if Demeter persisted in her mourning, called Hermes to him. "Go to Hades," he instructed his messenger, "and tell him that he must relinquish Kore and send her back to her mother. Otherwise, there will be an end to everything beneath Olympus. Then go to Demeter, and say to her, 'Your daughter will be yours again unless she has eaten anything in the Kingdom of the Dead.'"

Hermes did as he was instructed, and when he reached the royal palace of bleak Tartarus, he found Kore in tears, seated beside her husband. When Hermes had delivered his message, Hades understood that he would have to surrender his wife to Zeus's will. She had refused to eat or drink at his table and was thin and pale. "I see I must lose you," he said to her. "But I tell you my longing for you will be as cruel as your mother's longing; and my arms will be as empty as hers. You are the queen of my darkness, Kore. I beg you not to remember me with loathing."

Kore gave him no answer; she was already on her feet. She flung back her head and let her black crown clatter to the floor. "Take me to my mother!" she exclaimed. Grimly Hades escorted her to the garden, where his chariot was waiting to carry her to the upper earth. But as she was climbing, one of the gardeners, Ascalaphus, came up and said to his master, "Your queen came into the garden one day, picked a crimson pomegranate, and split it open. She took seven seeds and ate them. I saw it with my own eyes."

"Then you will bear witness for me to her mother," said Hades, and had the man climb onto the back of the chariot. Hermes took the reins, and they sped upward till they broke through the crust of the earth and into the sunlight. Kore gasped with pleasure as she drank in the pure air of Eleusis, and again with joy when the chariot reached Demeter's temple. Kore and Demeter flew to each other and laughed and cried and would not be parted. But when Demeter heard the testimony of the gardener, her eyes grew dark. She bared her teeth and clung to Kore so fiercely that her nails nearly pierced the girl's flesh.

"My curse on the land forever," she roared, "if my daughter cannot be mine. Never again will I return to Olympus, where Zeus the betrayer dwells. I will remain here, in my temple, and watch the earth, and every lovely living thing upon it, perish."

Zeus heard her and knew he must bring himself to intervene at last. He called his mother, Rhea, who was also the mother of Hades and Demeter, and sent her down to Eleusis to reason with Demeter. "My child," said Rhea, "my own daughter, this is the decision of Zeus, who desires an end to your suffering. Come home with Kore to join the immortals on Olympus. Let the earth flower again, and the mortals upon it be nourished. But know that for six months of each year, Kore must return to her husband in Tartarus, and reign by his side as queen of the Kingdom of the Dead, where she will be called Persephone, bringer of destruction. In those months the earth will be cold and bleak, but when she comes back to you, it will flourish, the crop will grow and be harvested, and you will be worshiped once more with sacred and mysterious rites as the giver of grain and life."

"I bow to the decision of Zeus," said Demeter. "He has restored my daughter to me." And she returned with Kore to their home on Olympus.

But each year, when Hecate arrives to lead Kore back down to Hades, Demeter puts her curse upon the earth. For half a year it lies bleak and barren; and every spring, when Persephone throws off her crown and comes back to her mother, it is reborn.

MIDAS

The infant Midas lay on his back, sound asleep. "Listen to that child smacking his lips," whispered his mother, Ida. "He's dreaming of food." Bending over him tenderly, she was astonished to see a long line of ants marching up the side of his cradle, each one carrying a single grain of wheat, which it slipped into Midas's greedy mouth.

"What can this mean?" wondered Ida. Soothsayers were summoned, put their gray heads together, and muttered gravely. At last the most venerable sage announced,

"He shall have surfeit of all he loves best,
He'll dine upon gold, and in gold he will dress.
Down through the ages shall echo his fame,
And the reeds in the meadow will whisper his name."

The goddess was overwhelmed at the greatness that lay before her in the form of her chubby infant. She lavished great care upon him and even sought out Orpheus, that fabulous musician, to be his tutor when he grew older. But she never learned who sent those ants. No god or goddess ever took credit for the blessing—or the joke.

Midas grew up to be a rather foolish, pleasure-loving king. He relished a good party and tended to blurt out whatever came into his head, particularly when he'd had an extra jug or two of wine. He surrounded his palace with rose gardens upon which he greatly prided himself, and he kept a crew of gardeners to tend them. One day these gardeners discovered an aged satyr sprawled snoring in a bower of roses, his fat belly prettily sprinkled with fallen petals. "Oho," they called, "what have we here? A sleeping princess?" And they bound him with garlands, and presented him to Midas for his amusement.

Midas recognized the drunken fellow at once as the foster father of the wine god, Bacchus. "Welcome, my dear Silenus," said he. "You seem to have strayed from Bacchus's protection, so I will offer you my own."

"Accepted!" crowed the old man, and proceeded to regale his host with tales of marvelous beings and enchanted lands, for he was a famous storyteller. Midas, in turn, poured the finest wines and served the most succulent dishes for his guest, and for ten days and nights they romped and roistered together. On the eleventh day Midas brought Silenus back home to Bacchus, who received both of them joyfully.

"I've been worried about the old goat," said Bacchus, "and I thank you for having treated him so grandly. You deserve a handsome reward—whatever you wish. Just name it."

Without stopping a second to consider, King Midas exclaimed, "All my life, dear Bacchus, I have cherished a marvelous dream in which everything I touched was turned to gold."

The god shook his head and replied,

> "Some things are better dreamed than had;
> Some gifts can drive the getter mad.
> What fancy paints so bright and fair,
> The light of day may foul—beware!"

But Midas insisted, and the wish was granted.

The king made his way home, ecstatic with his new gift. He plucked a toadstool and it became a golden ornament. He picked up a stone; it turned to gold. He kicked gleefully with his golden shoes at a clod of monkey dung, and it, too, shone buttery gold. There would be no end to his wealth! He would live in a gorgeous glittering world. When he entered the castle he gave it a golden door, and he fairly danced through the rooms, turning everything, even the humble chamber pots, to precious metal. Famished by these exertions, he sat himself down at the table and called for a feast of celebration. A tender nightingale's breast was set before him. The first bite chipped his tooth. He spat out the cold, hard lump in horror, and he reached for his wine glass, but the wine turned to a river of gold, and he nearly choked on it.

Just then his little daughter ran into the room, laughing and calling, "Papa, Papa, the house is so full of wonderful things!" And she would have rushed straight into his arms, but he shrank away from her, terrified, for now he realized how much his rash wish had cost him. No food could ever nourish him, nothing would quench his thirst. And worst of all, he had lost forever the warmth of a human touch.

The child sobbed in bewilderment to be so rebuffed. "No, no, don't cry, my dear one. I am ill, and I don't want to give you my sickness," said the king. Then he rushed from the palace and straight to Bacchus, imploring him, "Please, forgive my greediness, and take back this gift. Now I see that it will deprive me of everything I love and even rob me of my life."

Bacchus laughed when he saw the king squirming inside his stiff golden clothes. "Go, my poor friend, to the river Pactolus, and follow it to its source. Bathe yourself in those waters, and

you will be freed of your good fortune. But remember, henceforth, to be careful what you wish for."

Midas dashed off to do as he was told, and when he reached the river's source, he threw himself headfirst under it. His golden touch was washed away, and the sands of Pactolus were turned to gold.

We may learn from a bit of foolishness, but there is always foolishness of a different kind waiting for us. So it was with Midas. He moved to the country, for he could no longer bear the sight of gold and riches, and there he lived modestly with his family. He had a small vegetable garden, which he tended himself, and he took to worshiping the rural god, Pan, and enjoying long, healthful walks in the fields and forests.

But one day Pan got it into his head that he was as fine a musician as Apollo and challenged him to a contest. The mountain god Tmolus was appointed judge, and a great many people, Midas among them, gathered to watch what promised to be a fine entertainment. Pan took the first turn. He played them a lively rustic tune, and the crowd tapped their toes, bobbled their heads, and snapped their fingers. Then it was Apollo's turn. The moment he touched his silver lyre, no one was able to move. Indeed, his listeners almost forgot to breathe, so entranced were they by the celestial harmonies his fingers drew from its strings. Tmolus immediately awarded the victory to Apollo, and everyone cheered his decision—except Midas. Despite Orpheus's tutelage, Midas knew nothing about music, but knew what he liked, and did not hesitate to assert indignantly that Pan's offering had been vastly superior. What was the man thinking of? Even he should have known better than to side with a simple rustic god over the great sun god himself.

"My good fellow," said Apollo, with a dazzling smile, "if you want to make an ass of yourself, do let me help you." Then Midas felt his ears tingling, and when he put his hands to his head, he found that he had grown a handsome set of long, hairy ass's ears, in place of his own. "There, now," laughed Apollo, "you have ears to suit your musical taste."

Midas had a special cap made to conceal his shameful state, but soon enough he was in need of a haircut, and there was no way he could conceal the deformity from his barber. "What you have seen," Midas told the man, "you have not seen. If you know what I mean."

"Certainly, sir," replied the barber cheerfully.

"On pain of death," added Midas. And the barber swore that he would tell no one. But the secret hummed in his head day and night, till he could think of nothing else, and felt that if he did not speak it, he would go mad. So he went to the river-bank, dug a hole, put his mouth down to it, and whispered into the silent earth,

> "A preposterous thing has come to pass—
> King Midas wears the ears of an ass."

Over and over he whispered the words, and when he felt that they had indeed left him and gone to dwell in the hole, he covered it up again and went home with a light heart.

But in the spring tall reeds sprang up, and when the wind passed among them they whispered Midas's humiliating secret to one another and to all who strolled there. Midas himself, walking one day by the riverbank, heard his monstrous condition betrayed to all the world. In a fury he condemned the barber to death. Then he called for an ox to be slain, filled a cup with its blood, drank it, and died. It is said that the wind still coaxes his secret from the whispering reeds.

DAPHNE AND APOLLO

Apollo was sauntering through the woods, plucking at his golden harp and composing a song in honor of his most recent triumph, when he came upon Cupid, the young son of Venus, goddess of love. The boy was perched on a boulder, amusing himself with his little bow and arrows.

"Infant," said Apollo, with a curl of his handsome lip, "who can you possibly think you are, to be making toys of my noble weapons? Surely you know that I alone am the god of archery? Haven't you heard how I slew the death-dealing, poisonous Python? He was so long that when he uncoiled himself, the tip of his tail rested at one end of the plains, while his head was nestled at the other. How dare you mimic my greatness?"

Cupid, not at all perturbed, laughed gleefully down at Apollo.

"Slayer of serpents, and god of humility,
No one dares question your archer's ability.
Still, it behooves you, great god, to take heed—
One infant arrow is all I will need!
Take it to heart, and take it from me,
You'll fall madly in love with the next girl you see."

So saying, he plucked from his tiny quiver a golden arrow and with it he pierced Apollo through the heart. Then the boy drew a second arrow, this one blunt and tipped with lead.

"She whom my second arrow strikes,
Will be immune to love's delights,"

he chortled. And as he giggled over Apollo's dismay, a deer fled out of the woods with the nymph Daphne racing after it. Cupid's arrow went straight through her heart.

This Daphne was loved and desired by many young men, whose hot words earned them nothing but cold looks; she had no use for them. Her only passion was to run free in the woods. Her father, Peneus, the river god, despaired of persuading her to choose a mate. "You might consider my situation," he implored. "Have I no right to a son-in-law? Am I to have no grandsons to dandle on my godly knees?"

But Daphne was revolted by the thought of marriage. "Forgive me, dearest father," she said, "I would rather be dinner for a wild boar than surrender my freedom to some silly, arrogant boy. I shall live like Diana, the virgin hunter. No man was ever her master. No man shall ever be mine!"

And her father, who adored her, said, "Do as your heart tells you. But I fear that your own beauty will be the enemy of your dreams."

"I am slain!" groaned Apollo. Stricken by the god's first golden arrow, he was torn by love. Daphne's short dress fluttered about her bare arms and bramble-scratched legs; her hair tumbled loose and wild about her damp cheeks and down upon her shoulders. Her lips were parted in ardor for the chase, and her eyes glittered with joy. The heedless girl took no notice whatever of him.

Apollo lusted for her, as she for the fleeing deer; and in his imagination he transformed her. What a magnificent creature! She would be perfect dressed in a charming gown, with her hair tamed under a little golden circlet.

"Stop, Daphne," he called. "Do not flee from me as though I were some common, cloddish boy.

"Behold me, Apollo, the god of brightness,
Lord of Delphi, the son of Jupiter.

I am the god of music and poetry,
    Speaking the truth, foreseeing the future!"

"In that case," said Daphne, "you must know how much I despise you!" And she raced on, as though she were indeed pursued by a wild boar.

Apollo leaped after her, calling, "Stop, Daphne, stop! My heart is breaking for fear you might stumble on a root or stone and bruise that delectable flesh."

"Disgusting!" called Daphne, as she ran on in terror. She covered her ears, but the god's words slipped like oil between her fingers.

"My darling Daphne, please slow down, you will surely damage yourself," shouted the god. Cupid, from his rocky perch, tossed his curls and laughed to see his game in play. And again the god called out,

> "Stay! Though I am the god of archery,
> Oh, what an arrow has pierced the heart of me,
> Daphne the fair!
> Pity the god of medicine, Daphne,
> I can't heal myself—oh please turn back to me!
> Only take care!"

"Apollo, you are the god of flatulence!" gasped Daphne.

Fleet as she was, the god, spurred by the sight of her thin dress and bare legs, was swifter. He did not slow his pace but ran faster, even as he reassured her. "Daphne, just let me hold you for one moment. Stop and rest in my arms!"

The exhausted girl felt his breath upon her neck and knew she had lost. One final effort brought her to the edge of the forest, where her father's river lay glittering before her. Sinking to the ground, she cried out to the river god, "Oh, Father, if you

love your daughter, please help me! Release me from this body that has indeed betrayed me!" Even as the words flew from her lips, she felt her limbs begin to stiffen and grow numb. Roots grew from her feet into the ground beneath her, and the sweet flesh Apollo had so hungered for was locked in bark.

"Ah, my poor daughter, you are saved," came the voice of the river god, Peneus. "The woods you love are yours. No brutal man shall ever be your master. My waters shall sustain you, and my grandchildren will be the little birds that shelter in your limbs." Daphne heard her father's voice. She smiled, and then her face was drowned in the bright laurel leaves that were her hair.

Apollo stood bereft, amazed, as though he, too, were rooted there. At last he reached his hand to stroke the new-formed bark, rested his forehead on the slender tree, and kissed its wood. "Daphne, beloved," whispered the god, "though you are lost, you shall be mine forever. Your leaves shall deck my quiver and my harp; they shall be woven into crowns for victors' brows. You'll know no seasons but be always green, even as I, Apollo, am forever young." And the slim leaves trembled, as the mournful river wind sighed through them.

LEDA

Clear and vibrant, the reflected sky rippled in the river Eurotas, upon whose grassy bank lay Leda, dreaming, as she so often did, of love. A white cloud, the merest thought of a cloud, appeared above her. Leda, seeking a shape for it, found a bird. She drew it down, or it fell, wide-winged, directly into her arms. Leda laughed. A swan! It was Zeus, of course. He could never resist a mortal woman, especially one so agreeably sprawled on a bed of myrtle under the Spartan sky. He had seldom been as ardently received.

A foaming of feathers, a churning of wings and limbs—it was done, he was gone. Gods feel no need to linger after love. "Rude," murmured Leda. "And highly unsatisfactory."

She rose, adjusted her draperies, and made straight for home, where she found her husband, King Tyndareus, taking

his afternoon nap. With a feather still caught in her hair, she surprised and delighted him.

Leda, in the fullness of time, gave birth to a pair of exceedingly large eggs. From the first, a fine set of mortal twins, Castor and Clytemnestra, were born. The second egg was as blue as the sky had been on that day by the riverbank. From it were hatched a pair of infant immortals, Pollux and Helen. The boys, Castor and Pollux, loved each other so much that eventually Zeus made a constellation, the Gemini, of them.

But the girls turned out to be troublesome. Clytemnestra married Agamemnon and murdered him—with the help of her lover, Aegisthus. And it was Helen, beautiful Helen, whose inclination toward love would one day lead her to betray her husband, Menelaus, run off with Paris, and kindle the fires that led to the Trojan War.

"The egg," clucked Leda, "doesn't fall far from the hen."

PYGMALION

Pleasure seekers loved the Cyprian town of Amathus, famous for its riches, its arts, and its women. Venus had her temple there, and visitors were warned to be wary of her ardent devotees: those reckless girls who wore horned caps upon their heads, and at whose savage rites an unsuspecting guest might become the unfortunate centerpiece.

Rumors of such wild rituals only lent spice to the place. More enticing still were other bands of carefree lusty girls who refused to worship Venus and were always ready for a bit of amorous revelry.

The goddess was offended by all of them. Eventually, her patience exhausted, she decided to leave the island altogether. "But on second thought," she said, "why should I be driven from the place I love? And why should I punish the whole of innocent Cyprus for the wickedness of a few?"

So first she turned her attention to ridding Amathus of the depraved Horned Girls, whose bloody worship was an insult to her. Confronting them before their altar, she proclaimed,

> "Great barbarous brutes you are—
> On four legs you shall run,
> Real horns shall crown your heads,
> Be bulls now, every one!"

And so they were. The women became a herd of bulls and ran off into the countryside, bellowing in terror.

For those frolicsome women who refused to worship her, Venus devised a more subtle punishment:

> "You, who leave my altar flameless,
> Sluts, who take your pleasures, shameless,
> What you did for sheer enjoyment
> Let it be your harsh employment.
> Do not think you can defy me.
> If you think I'm joking, try me."

And she turned them into whores. What they had done for the sport of it, they were now obliged to do for pay. No woman had ever sold her body before Venus invented this curious punishment. But that was not enough for the goddess. When she saw that her victims continued to relish the pleasure as well as the pay, and to deny her divinity as well, she hardened them, body and soul. Their ardor cooled, resentment made them heavy and slow, the blood solidified in their veins, and they became stone monuments to her wrath.

There was in Amathus a sculptor named Pygmalion, who worshiped Venus almost to the point of madness. With equal intensity he loathed the easy, breezy girls who teased him for his priggishness. They called endearments after him when he passed by with a scowl, his eyes averted; they flipped their little skirts to see him blush. He lived a hermit's life; no womanly head had ever graced his pillow. "Nature," said he, "has done a bad job with women. They are lascivious, bloodthirsty creatures, bent solely on the abuse and corruption of mankind. I'll have none of them. Art will be my only love."

But he was young and lonely, and his art knew better than he did where the truth lay. It compelled him to fashion a woman—a woman perfect beyond the possibility of human flesh—an ivory Venus. And he worshiped her, could not keep his hands off her, caressed her virginal limbs, laid his cheek against her full pale breasts, traced with his finger their delicate nipples, whispered constantly, adoringly, "Dearest, oh, my dearest love."

He offered her gifts: pet birds to enchant her pretty ears, flowers to twine into her intricate hair. He graced her with ribbons, with amber beads and rings; he dressed her, and then

enjoyed the greater pleasure of undressing her, so that her ivory flesh glowed like the moon. Night after night he laid her gently on a bloodred coverlet and kissed her on the lips. "Warm to me," he implored her. "Love me. Live!" But she was icy, chaste, and hard. Not even the heat of his tears could move her to life. "Cold, cold woman," he threatened, "since you feel nothing, I shall smash you to marble dust!" And he would tear off her fripperies and shake his mallet viciously. Then he would weep, and beg forgiveness, and abase himself before her dainty feet. He intolerable love consumed him; he grew thin and forsook his work entirely.

The festival of Venus was an occasion for great festivity on Cyprus; the whole island turned out to worship and celebrate the goddess. When the time came around, Pygmalion sought her out. He pushed through crowds of celebrants, oblivious of the snowy heifers, destined to be sacrificed, with their dangerous, gold-tipped horns. He drew back, revolted, from the ecstatic girls who thronged Venus's temples, and found, at last, a place at an altar where, with other lovelorn youths and maidens, he made his offering, and prayed:

"Hear, oh goddess, the voice of thy servant, humble
     and dutiful.
Receive thou my offering, Venus, kindest, most beautiful.

Give me a wife like my ivory maiden, save me from
   madness.
Show me a sign, I pray, or let me perish of sadness."

   The goddess heard him. She saw into his inflamed heart
and understood what he dared not ask of her. It was not a girl
who resembled the ivory maiden that he desired, but the statue
herself. And Venus made the flame he had lit at her altar leap
up three times, as a sign for him.

   Pygmalion raced from the temple, shoved through the
riotous crowds and back to his studio, where his work lay, as
if sleeping, on her scarlet bedcloth. He lay down beside her,
timidly, fearfully, and placed his hand on the cold breast he had
fondled so many times, and this time he felt a small tremor
there, deep, where a heartbeat might be expected. The ivory
warmed to his hand, became flesh, responded to his touch. He
kissed her lips, now rosy; he caught up her hair and entangled
his fingers in tresses no longer frozen. "Beloved," he murmured,
"look at me." And her eyes, her blue eyes, looked back at him in
wonder. She smiled at him. "I am Pygmalion," he told her, "and
your name will be Galatea." And in his heart he whispered,
"Thank you, great Venus, my goddess."

EUROPA

Europa, King Agenor's daughter, struggled and wept. Two huge women were quarreling over her. "I am Asia," exclaimed the first. "I gave birth to you, girl, and you belong to me!" And she took hold of Europa's left arm, and pulled at it ferociously.

"You will be mine!" shrieked the other. "I have no name, but Zeus will give you to me, and I will take your name, as well!" And she pulled just as fiercely at Europa's right arm. The women began to swell, they were vast, they were continents. They would tear her in two.

Europa awoke in terror. It was dawn, the hour of prophetic dreams. Hurriedly she pulled on a purple dress and ran to find her friends. "Come out with me," she begged them. "I need to shake off my horrors. Let's go to that meadow nearest

52

the sea; I'll wash away my nightmare, and then we can fill our baskets with flowers." Europa held up her golden basket. It was a treasure in itself, made by Hephaestus, the metalsmith of the gods.

This Hephaestus was the only ugly member of the immortals. He was miserably scrawny at birth, and Hera, his mother, took one look at him and dropped him right off Mount Olympus into the sea. But Hephaestus managed to survive; indeed, he became so sublime a craftsman that Hera swallowed her pride and brought him back to Olympus. There she established him in a fine smithy and married him off to Aphrodite, who was constantly unfaithful to him. Hephaestus had a hard time of it with his celestial family. When he quarreled with Zeus, whom he reproached for hanging Hera from heaven by her wrists during a marital squabble, Zeus hurled him off Olympus again. This time he was an entire day falling, broke both his legs, and was lame ever after.

Hephaestus had engraved Europa's basket all around with scenes from the sad story of Io, a mortal maiden who was changed to a cow by Zeus in order to prevent Hera from discovering their flirtation. This extreme measure was not effective. Hera caught on to the affair and punished poor Io even further by setting a gadfly to tormenting her. It pursued her all over the world, biting at her hide, till at last she was restored to her natural form—a relatively happy ending for any tale involving gods and humans.

So there was Europa, with her precious basket in hand, and her friends with theirs. The girls ran down to the sea, where they bathed themselves, and Europa forgot her nightmare. Then they wandered to and fro in the meadow, calling out to each other,

"Violets!"

"Hyacinths!"

"Wild roses!" And they competed to see who would have the most, and bedecked each other till they looked like a dancing garden. Zeus himself peered down from Olympus to watch their revels, and Aphrodite spotted him. The goddess could never resist a tempting target for romantic mischief. She let fly one of her arrows; it found his heart, and he was smitten with Europa on the instant.

Fearing discovery by the ever-vigilant Hera, Zeus changed himself into a chestnut-colored bull. Then he summoned Hermes, his messenger. "Go quickly to Sidon," he said, "and drive King Agenor's cattle down to that seaside meadow, where the girls are so charmingly disporting themselves." And when it was done, he went among them in his disguise.

Europa was the first to discover him. "Look there!" she exclaimed. "That magnificent bull! I've never seen anything like him."

"He has a silver circle on his forehead!" marveled one of the girls.

"His horns are curved like young crescent moons!" called another.

Zeus, the bull, stared at them with his great brown eyes, and they were all entranced. Then he ambled to them, through the crocuses and violets.

"He's very gentle," they said. "He smells heavenly—sweeter than all the meadow flowers." And they began to pet him and make much of him and even to adorn him with their garlands. He let them play with him awhile.

"I do believe he's smiling," said Europa, and he nuzzled her tenderly. When she stroked his flanks he made such a soft, melodious sound that she embraced his great neck. Then the bull laid himself down at Europa's feet and tossed his head, as if inviting her to mount him.

"Look, girls," she said, "this beast is almost human. Let's make him give us a little ride." And she climbed up on his back. The others ran to join her, but Zeus was too quick for them. Before they had taken two steps, he leaped to his feet, raced to the shore, and with the stunned Europa on his back, went flying out over the water. The girl clung tightly to the bull's horn with one hand, still clutching her basket in the other, and drew up her feet to protect her sandals from the waves. She called out

to her friends, but her words were lost on the wind. The purple of her dress billowed out like a sail, and she disappeared from sight in a twinkling.

Europa gazed down in wonder at the marvelous creatures that rose from the ocean's depths to swim below her and her steed. There were Nereids, those nymphs of the sea, riding their dolphins; there was Triton, blasting on his huge shell trumpet; and Proteus, his form constantly changing. And then she saw great Poseidon himself, ruler of the waters, under whose golden chariot wheels the waves grew still. He had come to escort his brother, Zeus, on this latest escapade.

"What are you?" exclaimed Europa. "Surely you are no mere brute. If you are a god, have pity on a mortal girl, I beg you. Do not use me in the way gods do! Don't leave me alone to die in some wild, friendless place."

Then the bull spoke to her in a caressing voice.

"Come child, rejoice, my love will never fail.
Why should you sob, and shudder, and turn pale?
Though father, brothers, Mother Asia weep,
A glorious destiny is yours, in Crete."

Europa saw below her a tiny speck of green in the blue Aegean waters; it became an island, and the bull landed gently upon its soil. Four maidens, the seasons, ran out to greet them, and speaking soothingly to the tearful Europa, they dressed her in bridal clothes. They led her to a thicket of willows beside a little stream, where Zeus appeared to her—this time disguised as an eagle—and had his way with her.

"You'll bear three mighty sons, and leave your name
On the vast continent to which you came,"

he announced grandly. And then he left her.

When her father, King Agenor, learned of his daughter's abduction, he tore his hair, rent his royal robes, and called his five sons to him. "Go search for your sister across the wide world," he said, "and do not dare to return without her." They sailed at once, in different directions, and none of them ever returned; at least not during his lifetime. The most famous of Europa's brothers was Cadmus. On the advice of the Delphic Oracle he abandoned the search for his sister and followed a cow to the place where the exhausted animal fell to the ground, and there he founded the city of Thebes.

Europa's destiny was glorious, after all. The continent upon which she made her new home is called Europe, in her honor, and she married Asterius, the king of Crete, who adopted her sons. Sarpedon became the king of Milya, and Zeus granted him the privilege of living for three generations. Minos married Pasiphaë, who fell in love with a bull (not Zeus, this time). After his death Zeus made him, together with his brother Rhadamanthus, judges of the souls of the dead in Tartarus. So they were, as Zeus had promised, mighty in life and also in death. It was one of the few promises he ever kept.

VENUS AND ADONIS

The grandson of Pygmalion and Galatea, King Cinyras of Cyprus, had one daughter, Myrrha. She was a great beauty, courted by all the princes of Asia, but she was cold to their flattery, unmoved by their faces, bored by their fortunes. As quickly as they appeared, she sighed and waved them away. "But, dearest, what sort of man would please you?" asked her bewildered father.

"Only a man exactly like you," answered Myrrha, blushing and trembling. King Cinyras smiled at her sweetness. He could not know that his wretched daughter was desperately in love with him. She herself was horrified by this forbidden passion. She struggled against it, tossing in her bed, feverish with desire, cold with fear.

"Why am I made to suffer this way? Have the gods decreed

it? On Mount Olympus they think nothing of mating with their sisters and brothers! I might have been born in some other country, where daughters and fathers, mothers and sons, are encouraged to love each other. Why not? Or better to have been a beast! The cow and the bull never ask for introductions; the ram is delighted to couple with the ewe who bore him. Oh, you gods, I implore you—my thoughts are vile, but I don't want to be an evil sinner. If you will not help me, how shall I resist this unspeakable longing?"

The gods were not helpful. At last one night Myrrha could bear it no longer. She tied a scarf around her neck, fixed it to the door lintel, and tried to hang herself. As she fell, her old nurse, who was sleeping in the next room, heard the noise, ran in, and loosed the knotted sheet that gripped her neck. "How could anything be so terrible that you should want to take your own life?" gasped the woman. "Tell me what this great sorrow can be, and I will comfort you. If you have some secret trouble, I will help you. Believe me, there is nothing I would not do for you! Can it be some lowborn youth you are yearning for?"

But Myrrha could only groan and beat her head with her fists and claw at her heart as if she wanted to open her breast and release it. At last, though she clenched her teeth and bit her lips, the words slipped through them, the smallest whisper escaped, and made its way to the old nurse's ears. "My own mother's husband. . . ."

The woman dropped to the floor beside Myrrha; her legs would not support such dreadful knowledge. She sobbed and groaned till it seemed her gasps were death rattles. But at last she threw herself upon the girl and said, "If it must be, it will be; I will share your guilt to save your life."

And it happened that the festival of Demeter was at hand, during which, for nine days and nights, married women were forbidden to lie with their husbands. Myrrha's mother would be among these white-robed celebrants; her husband's bed would be empty. On the first night, the old woman went to him and said, "There is a young woman who is dying for love of you. Will you have her?"

"How old is she?" asked Cinyras.

"About Myrrha's age."

"Let her come," he said.

The old nurse first brought the king a goodly quantity of wine, saying lewdly, "This will fortify you for the delights to come." Then she went to Myrrha and led her to her father's bed. Evil omens attended them. An owl shrieked three times in warning. Three times Myrrha's reluctant feet stumbled, but they carried her across the threshold. "Take her," said the woman. "She is yours."

The night was dark, and the wine had done its work. The king had no idea who the young virgin might be who was so passionate, who said nothing, but sobbed so bitterly in his arms. She came to him night after night, never uttering a word, but signaling her love for him in a hundred intimate ways. At last, on the ninth night, his curiosity overcame him. He called for candles, and in a moment the light fell upon the despairing face of his own daughter. Cinyras's cry of rage and horror shook the palace. He leaped up and drew his sword to kill her.

Perhaps his love for her slowed his hand. The girl flew from his dishonored bed into the sheltering night. For nine months she wandered, wretched, far from her father's kingdom, while her belly grew big with her son, who was also her brother. When the time came, Myrrha, overwhelmed by the enormity of her crime, sick and weary of her life, called upon the gods once again:

> "Although I am not worthy, I pray you be kind,
> You gods. Find me the end I deserve.
> Though I do not merit the mercy of death,
> Alive, my flesh defiles the good earth,
> And my spirit would foul the Land of the Dead.
> Punish me, banish me now, to a state
> Less than human, utterly changed.
> Find me, kind gods, my fate."

And her prayer was answered. Her feet, weary with wandering, took root; bark embraced her, hid her from the world that loathed her crime. Leaves lidded her eyes. She became a myrrh tree. She wept still, but now her tears were bitter sap.

The child in her womb struggled for release. He kicked so violently that the bark burst open, and Adonis was born into the arms of Venus, who stood waiting to catch him. He was the loveliest infant imaginable; the goddess fell in love with him at once. She put him into a little wooden chest and brought it down to Tartarus, where she entrusted it to Persephone, saying, "Just tuck this box away for me, my dear. I'll be back for it in ten years or so."

How could Persephone resist a peek into the mysterious chest? When her eyes fell upon the baby she, too, fell in love with it. The infant became a boy, the boy became a wonderfully handsome youth, and Persephone, enchanted, took him for her lover.

Gossip travels quickly, especially among the gods and goddesses, who can fly anywhere in the wink of a knowing eye. Venus soon got wind of the affair in the dark kingdom, and rushed there to demand her pretty boy. But Persephone would not relinquish Adonis.

"He is mine," roared Venus. "You stole my child, and now you've seduced him. You have a husband, Hades. Why don't you produce a child of your own with which to divert yourself?"

"You locked the baby away in a chest," shouted Persephone. "You gave him to me and never cared an olive for him, until he grew up to be so beautiful."

Finally they were forced to appeal to Zeus to settle the matter. He ruled that each of them might have Adonis for half of the year: he would spend autumn and winter in the Land of the Dead with Persephone, and spring and summer on earth with the goddess of love.

Venus's lust was insatiable. She could not bear to lose sight of Adonis for a single hour when he was with her. Without a thought, she forsook her usual self-indulgent, comfort-loving ways, let her hair go loose in a wild tangle, and dressed in rough skins, as rudely as the huntress Diana. She raced with Adonis through the woods, with dogs, bows and arrows, and spears, allowing her perfect skin to be caressed by weeds and thorns in the pursuit of small game. But she was always haunted by the fear of losing her human lover. "Never, my dearest," she implored him, "go after the fierce animals, the ones with teeth and horns and claws—lions or boars that might tear at your flesh. You must hunt only those that have no means of self-protection. Birds, for example, and rabbits."

Adonis rebelled against these restrictions. He longed to assert his own will, and one day when his hounds flushed a wild boar

them he fashioned two elegant pairs of wings, to be attached by an ingenious system of straps. Daedalus tested them carefully, and found them as serviceable as the wings of the gulls after which they had been modeled. Greatly satisfied with his work, he bound the smaller set to the arms of his son, and that night he showed Icarus how to fly. At first they made short flights, staying close to the ground. Then they ventured a little higher, and by the time the sun had risen, Daedalus felt that Icarus had learned his lesson well. He embraced the lad and kissed him tenderly, saying,

"Icarus, heed me. You will never hear
Words of more gravity. Be sure your flight
Is measured by my own. Stay close, my son,
Do not permit the power and delight
You'll feel to draw you on too high. The sun
Will melt these waxen wings, and you will fall;
Nor dip too near the sea—the water's weight
Will make them heavy, and the waves will call
You to them. Trust in me, mind what I say,
And we'll be free of Crete this very day."

"Father, they are wonderful wings," said Icarus. "Don't be afraid. I will follow close to you and do exactly as you have told me."

Then father and son spread their wings and raced along the sand till the wind bore them up. They rose and flew. Below them, plowmen straightened their backs to stare at the sky, shepherds forgot their flocks for a moment, fishermen let their lines go slack, and women allowed the water to flow from the mouths of their jars as they gazed up openmouthed and whispered a prayer, sure that these must be gods on their mysterious errands.

Young Icarus was enraptured by such freedom, intoxicated by the wish to fly even higher, oh, yes, to fly even as high as a god. His father forgotten, all danger forgotten, he spread his wings wide and soared joyfully toward the sun.

Daedalus, peering back over his shoulder, saw the boy on his upward course and called out to him, "Icarus!" But the air swallowed his words, as the sun melted the wax and the sea swallowed his son, leaving only a little halo of feathers to show where the water had received him. Daedalus could only weep and fly on, his salt tears falling into the blue water.

ARACHNE

Minerva, goddess of wisdom, inventor of olives, and tamer of horses, sat contentedly in her garden, working at her loom. She was also the goddess of arts and prided herself particularly on her weaving. No one had ever come near to matching her skill. Her fabrics were gossamer, and the scenes she wove into them were so vivid that when the slightest breeze teased them the figures seemed to come alive.

There was a sudden, small commotion at her gate, and a group of mischievous nymphs ran in crying, "Beloved goddess, have you happened to hear of Arachne? She's a little nobody, simply a dyer's daughter, but her weavings and embroideries are so exquisite, some even dare to say that they rival yours. And you ought to see how gracefully she works! The slightest movement of her hands is a delight, even when she is only carding or spinning. Everyone is enchanted with her. When we asked if you had given her lessons, she glared at us furiously and said, "What a stupid idea! I was born to weave. I never needed a teacher at all, not even a goddess. And if Minerva thinks she is superior, fine—let her come and show us. I challenge her to a contest. If I lose, I swear I will pay her price, whatever it is!"

Minerva, who had jumped, full-grown and resplendent in armor, straight out of Jupiter's forehead, was as ferocious a warrior as her father, and she alone among his children was allowed to carry his shield and his terrible thunderbolt. Now she leaped up and stamped her foot. Then she sat down and poked out her lips. Then she folded them in and stared for a while at her nose. At last she snorted, sprang up again, and demanded to know where that impudent Arachne might be found. The nymphs, covering their naughty smiles, were quick to point the way.

The goddess transformed herself into a lame old woman, and with a cane in her hand and her pet owl on her shoulder, she appeared before Arachne. "Well, dearie," said she, "I've been hearing so much about you, I thought I might just as well see what all the commotion's about, and give you a bit of useful advice while I'm at it."

"Thank you," replied Arachne. "I'm doing very nicely on my own."

"So far," said the woman, "so far. But I've learned a great deal in my long, long life, and you might as well hear me out:

> "That fool who with the goddess vies,
> Catastrophe shall be her prize:
> However fair the web she spin,
> She'll be the one who's caught therein.
> Repent, rash girl, and bow your head;
> Your future hangs on just one thread.
> The choice is this: to eat your pride,
> Or dine on beetles, gnats, and files."

"I detest riddles," said Arachne, "so keep your advice to yourself, you witless old meddler, or pass it along to your poor daughters-in-law. I know my worth, and I won't play dumb. I'm not afraid of the goddess; why should I be? She must have heard of me. Let her come down from Olympus and prove herself. If she dares."

"SHE COMES!" thundered Minerva. The crone vanished, and in her place stood the goddess, her gray eyes flashing.

The nymphs dropped to their knees, and the women who were gathered around shrank back, trembling in terror. But not Arachne. First she turned red, and frowned. Then she turned white, and glared. Then she laughed out loud. "Very well, goddess," said she, "let us find out who is supreme!"

With a toss of her chin Minerva caused two looms to appear, and the contestants sat down to their work. Each had at her side great heaps of the most exquisite wool in every hue, from the subtlest to the most vibrant, and gold and silver as well. These threads were so wonderfully fine that the webs seemed wrought with skeins of luminous sea spray.

The rivals wove quickly, with great passion, their fingers flying, their eyes darting often at each other's work. Minerva filled her loom with the twelve great gods of Olympus, as they sat in judgment on her own triumphant contest with Neptune. At the four corners she showed the terrible fate of mortals who had dared to challenge a god, each a cautionary tale for her rival. To make sure that her point was taken, she named them, as if to herself:

> "Two who took the names of gods
> Were turned to mountains, silly clods.
> And here's a girl with little brain—
> She angered Juno. She's a crane.
> Lower left, Antigone,
> Became a stork, as you can see.

Cinyras's daughters, upper right,
Now temple steps. Pathetic sight."

If Arachne understood these images as a warning to give up her dangerous contest, she showed no sign. She, too, took the gods for her subject, and there was something defiant and disrespectful in the tilt of her head, in the very manner of her weaving, even in the extraordinary, intricate wreath of flowers and vines that bordered it. She, too, murmured as she worked:

"Oh, yes, we mortals are aware
How gods abuse the young and fair.
How Jupiter, to cool his lust,
Rolled many a maiden in the dust.
Disguised as swan, or bull, or flame,
Or shower of gold, or snake—he came.
And Neptune, great Apollo, too,
Amused themselves with quite a few—
Tricked out as river, lion, ram,
Without so much as 'thank you, ma'am.'"

When they had finished, no one dared say which tapestry was the more marvelous; it was clear that goddess and mortal were equals. Arachne tied off her fragile web and arose with a smug, triumphant smile. Minerva, in a fury at this display of arrogance, plunged her nails into the offending work and ripped it to shreds from top to bottom. Then she seized her shuttle and beat Arachne so mercilessly about the head that the mortified girl, unable to bear her own rage and humiliation, ran into the woods and hanged herself.

When Minerva saw her dangling there she could not help but feel a little pity. "Insolent mortal," she said, "foolhardy girl. I'll let you live, and you may even keep the weaver's skill that's cost you dearly. But you will not forget this lesson from a goddess:

"You, who thought yourself so clever,
You shall dangle there forever.
All your children, all your kind,
Shall hang, until the end of time."

With that she reached under her cloak and drew out a cup filled with deadly wolfsbane. She dashed the poisonous stuff straight into Arachne's eyes, and at once the girl moaned pitifully and retuned to life. But what a terrible gift! Her hair fell out, her nose and her ears dropped off like ripe berries, her head became small as the head of a pin. Her body dwindled to nothing, her fingers stuck to her sides and turned into bent, hairy

legs, as skinny as wire. Then from the center of her shrunken ball of a belly she spun one single thread, finer than anything she had ever spun before. She hangs from it still: Arachne—a spider trapped in a web of her own weaving.

HERO AND LEANDER

L eander, his hair still damp with sea spray, peered into the charming little temple. He had just come from Abydos, the Asian town across the Hellespont, and had an idle hour to pass before returning home. A young priestess, Hero, spied him, and beckoned him inside, saying,

"Venus welcomes you."

"Hail to her. And do you welcome me, too?"

"That is my duty."

"As love is hers." And they went on like that; it hardly mattered what they said. There were looks and smiles and something unspoken that was agreed upon before he left. In a few days he came again, and then again, and their love grew, though the temple was seldom without other worshipers of

Venus, and there was never more than an hour before he had to leave her.

One day Hero said to him, "The strait is so narrow you could almost spit across it, but it will keep us apart forever."

"Nothing can do that," he answered. "This boat is not mine, but tonight I will come to you. Light a torch and set it on that tower; then watch for me. Have no fear; I will not fail you."

No one had ever swum across the Hellespont because of the relentless current from the Sea of Marmora into the Archipelago. "It must be," thought Hero, "that he will find another boat." So she lit a torch that night and climbed the tower, and fixed it there. Then she hurried to the shore, and let the small waves lap at her toes while she listened for the splash of his oars. So intent was she upon that sound that she did not see him till he rose suddenly from the waves and stood laughing with his arms upraised like Neptune, god of the sea. Amazed, Hero flew into his arms, drenched as he was, and pulled him to the temple, where together they celebrated the goddess of love.

Each night thereafter Hero lit the torch and waited for her lover, and each night he came to her. But one night the sky grew dark, hard rain fell, and a tempest blew up. "What shall I do?" she wondered. "Of course he does not mean to come.

"He will not be so foolhardy, surely.
But then, he does love me most truly.
If I don't light the torch, he will heed me.
But suppose he so desperately needs me
That he sets off in darkness, all blindly?
I must guide him, so he will come find me."

And she argued back and forth with herself, but in the end her longing was stronger than her reason, and she climbed the tower, fearfully, because of the great wind that had sprung up, and planted her torch. Then she struggled to the temple, to shelter awhile till she might expect him. From the temple door she could not see the dark tower, or know that her torch had guttered and blown out.

Hero waited awhile, and when she could wait no longer she went down to the shore and paced along the sand, peering out across the water to Abydos. No path of light shone across the waves, as it had always done. She turned her head and saw there was no torch burning upon the tower, and when she turned back in terror to the sea, she stumbled upon something lying on the sand at her feet. The waves had carried Leander to her for the last time. She bent and seized his hands; they were cold as death. Salt glittered on his lips where she kissed him again and again, crying,

"Beloved, my light has gone out,
But have no fear.
I will join you once more, in the dark,
Oh, wait, my dear!"

Then she took a small knife she carried with her and
plunged it deep into her breast; and her warm body fell upon
his cold one, in a last embrace.

Venus, goddess of love, took no part in this story, though it was in her temple at Sestos that the lovers met. It is only a simple tale, moved not by vain or lustful gods with all their shenanigans, but only by nature, both human and elemental— as dangerous, in the end, as any jealous Olympian.

PERSEUS

King Acrisius of Argos had a spirited daughter, Danaë, but he longed for a son—one who would look just like him, and would, under his tutelage, become a noble ruler when Acrisius decided to retire. He traveled to Delphi to consult Apollo's oracle about his chances. But the news was not good. Indeed, the priestess terrified him, saying,

"Of male children you shall have none,
But you shall be slain by your own daughter's son."

Acrisius knew that the gods never looked kindly upon those who slew their blood relations, so he did not have his daughter killed, as he was tempted to do, but sealed her up in a dungeon with brass walls and set fierce dogs to guard her. "No man will find you here," he told her. "No man will have the chance to father my murderer." This was true enough—but in the roof of the dungeon there was a little skylight, and one day Zeus, with his ever-wandering eye, caught sight of her and visited her, fancifully disguised as a shower of gold.

By and by Danaë bore a son, whom she called Perseus. When King Acrisius learned of the birth, he was beside himself with anger and demanded to know who the father might be.

"Zeus," explained Danaë. "He came through the skylight, in a golden rain."

"Wretched, treacherous girl," raged Acrisius, "how can you insult me with such a ridiculous tale? I dare not have your blood on my hands, but the wild waves will do my work for me." And fearing the fulfillment of the Delphic prophecy, he locked Danaë and her infant son in a large wooden chest and cast it into the sea.

Storm-tossed and despairing, Danaë clung to her child, certain that they would both be drowned; but the chest was carried safely to the island of Seriphos, where a fisherman, Dictys, brought it up in his net. When he discovered Danaë and Perseus inside, he led them at once to his brother, King Polydectes.

"The poor things," said Polydectes, "they can stay for as long as they like." Then he dismissed them to a faraway wing of his house and didn't give either of them a thought for years. One day, however, as he was strolling in the garden he chanced upon Danaë, sitting on a little stone bench eating a fig, her lips and fingers sticky with its juice. She was still a fine-looking woman, and Polydectes was suddenly smitten with love for her. "You will be my wife," he declared.

"I'm quite content as I am," replied Danaë. The king persisted. But when he tried to force her to marry him, Perseus, now a young man, defended his mother against these unwanted attentions, and Polydectes decided to rid himself of the youth.

The king pretended to lose interest in Danaë. He summoned his closest companions and said, "Good friends, I am a lonely man, and it is my dearest wish to take a wife. Seriphos is a small place, and I have no great wealth to lure a woman to it, but I know you will be eager to help me find happiness. If each of you would only contribute one fine horse, I would have a handsome gift to offer my bride." He called upon them one by one, and one by one, however reluctantly, they agreed. "And beloved Perseus," he added, "surely I can count on you?"

Perseus was relieved to learn that Polydectes no longer desired his mother. He had neither horse nor money, but he was a proud fellow, as the king was well aware, and he fell right into the trap the sly Polydectes had set for him. He offered something he knew the king longed for. "Sir," he said, "I have nothing to give for your good lady but my wits and my strength, and with these I swear I will contrive to slay Medusa, the Gorgon, and bring her head to you." Polydectes could not have been more delighted. The troublesome boy had just volunteered to go off and get himself killed.

Medusa had once been a beautiful young girl, so beautiful that she was compared to the goddess Athene, particularly because of her magnificent mop of bright curly hair. This was her misfortune, as Athene, too, was renowned for her hair, and she could never bear to be challenged in anything. The minute she heard of her rival she went to her. "Let's see what compliments you will enjoy now, presumptuous girl!" she hissed.

"Your tongue shall swell, your teeth as well,
With tusks of swine your jaws be lined,
Brass claws, instead of fingernails
You'll wear, and awful, golden scales.
Huge wings your shoulder bones shall bear,
And as for that once dazzling hair—
A mass of poisonous snakes, instead,
Shall take possession of your head."

And Athene changed the girl into a Gorgon. Medusa was now so hideous that any living creature who looked upon her was frozen at once into stone. She went to live with her two Gorgon sisters somewhere—in a cave, on an island—no one knew exactly where, and no one wished to know. King Polydectes could be quite sure that Perseus, if he managed to find her, would become a statue of himself.

Now it was Perseus's turn to set sail for Delphi, to ask the oracle where Medusa made her home. The priestess answered,

"Where men eat acorns and trees speak,
Look for a clue to what you seek."

So he went on to Dodona, where men made bread from acorn flour and the oak trees spoke the will of Zeus.

"This we can say—the future shades the rest:
Know, traveler, that the gods smile on your quest,"

they whispered. But they were unable to tell him where Medusa lived.

Then Athene, whose hatred for Medusa had never left her, appeared at Perseus's side. "Brave and virtuous youth," she declared, "I will aid you in your mission. But if you let your eye fall upon Medusa or her sisters you will be petrified in an instant; and while you would certainly make a handsome statue, Medusa would remain alive. Take this bright shield, which I carry for my father, Zeus, to protect you. Be sure to look only at Medusa's reflection in it, and you will be spared."

Next, the god Hermes, messenger of Zeus, came to Perseus. He was a glorious young man, with wings on his sandals, his wand, and his hat. "I will guide you," he said, "for the way to your goal is long and twisting. And I will lend you my adamantine sword. Not even the Gorgon's scales can deflect its blade. But first we must go to the Graeae, the Gray Women, who are also Medusa's sisters, and force them to tell us how to find the Nymphs of the North, who hold the last three things you will need to slay the Medusa: winged sandals, a magic wallet that is always exactly the right size for what is to be carried in it, and a helmet of invisibility."

Perseus and Hermes traveled together a long way, to the misty land at the foot of Mount Olympus where the three Gray Women sat on their thrones. Their bodies were shaped like swans, but their heads were human, and they had both wings and arms. They shared one single tooth and a single eye, which they handed back and forth continually. Perseus, on the advice of the cunning Hermes, stole up behind them, and when one of the creatures took the eye and the tooth from her head to pass to her sister, he snatched them from her, crying,

"Hunger and darkness are yours henceforth,
Till you show me the road to the Nymphs of the North!"

"Go then, go to the country of the Hyperboreans, who dwell at the back of the north wind. No man can find that place, not by land and not by water. But you shall take that wondrous road, dear sir—only give us our precious eye and tooth." And they pointed the way with trembling fingers.

Perseus gave back the eye and the tooth, and with the god still guiding him, journeyed to the back of the north wind. In that warm and sunny land, which lay close to the home of the muses, there were neither sickness nor old age. The pleasure-loving Hyperboreans danced all day to the sound of the flute and lyre and feasted merrily each night. Perseus and Hermes were invited to join in the revels while the obliging nymphs went off to fetch what Perseus required. He put on the winged sandals and the helmet of invisibility. Then armed with the magic silver wallet, Hermes's invincible sword, and Athene's shield, he and Hermes flew back over the ocean to the island of the Gorgons.

The Terrible Sisters were asleep in their cave, surrounded by the petrified forms of those who had had the evil fortune to look upon them. Each face wore an expression of indescribable terror. Perseus steeled himself against these horrors, and, gazing into the mirror of his shield, he beheld the Gorgons, with their great wings, their glittering, golden scales, the hissing snakes of their hair. For an instant he hovered over Medusa. Then, with

90

one savage stroke of his sword, he severed her head from her body. Grasping the still-seething hair, he dropped the head into his wallet. Medusa's sisters awoke and thrashed their wings, but he was invisible; they could not find him.

Then Hermes turned to Perseus and said,

"I leave you now, for the prize is won.
Your wits shall guide you the long way home."

So Perseus set off to return to Seriphos. On his way there he flew over Ethiopia, where he spied a maiden chained, naked, to a rocky ledge. This girl, Andromeda, was waiting to be devoured by a monstrous sea serpent because her mother, Cassiopeia, had thoughtlessly offended the Nereids, and worse yet, their protector, Poseidon. The sea god demanded that Andromeda be sacrificed in this cruel fashion, in expiation of the insult. Perseus alit beside the trembling girl and fell in love with her at once. When the monster reared its horrid head to seize her, he struck it off with his sword, unchained Andromeda, and carried her triumphantly home to her parents.

"Rejoice," he said to them. "Here is your daughter, alive; and here is the head of the monster to whom you abandoned her. I claim her as my bride. Take her and dress her for our wedding."

The parents had no choice. They clad Andromeda in exquisite bridal clothes and prepared a magnificent nuptial feast, with much raillery and drinking of toasts. Suddenly a vast army burst into the hall. At its head was Agenor, the king's twin

With your tales and your clever retorts—
You may have the last word, but no more!"

Echo opened her mouth to defend herself against the goddess's anger, but she found she could only wail, "No more!" And from that moment, she could never offer a sentence of her own, but only give back what was spoken to her.

Nevertheless, she burned with love for Narcissus, and she was determined to seduce him. One day she followed him secretly as he was hunting in the woods with some companions. She hoped she might have the good luck to catch him alone and fling herself into his arms. Indeed she was lucky, for Narcissus became separated from the other youths and called out, "Is anyone here?"

"Here!" exclaimed Echo.

"Then come to me," called Narcissus.

"Come to me!" returned Echo.

Narcissus, bewildered, gazed about him. Seeing no one, he became angry; he was not used to being ignored. "Why are you playing with me?" he demanded. "Let's get together." Those were just the words Echo longed to say.

"Let's get together," she cried, and sprang from her hiding place with her arms already shaped to embrace her beloved. But the youth drew back, and she saw him shudder in revulsion.

"Don't you touch me," he hissed.

This cruelty was even more painful to Echo than Hera's spiteful punishment. "You . . . touch . . . me," she whispered, and covered her flaming face with her hands. Then she turned and fled into the woods. That was the last anyone ever saw of her. She wandered through wild and lonely places, wasting away with shame and longing. Her flesh dried and shriveled from her bones, the bones themselves turned to mountain stone, and nothing remained of Echo, only her voice.

There were many other admirers who suffered the cold sting of Narcissus's scorn. At last one rejected youth felt his humiliation so keenly that he prayed to Nemesis, goddess of vengeance, saying, "O just goddess, let Narcissus know this torment: let him weep, and burn, and never be granted the love of the one he yearns for."

The goddess was listening. One day Narcissus, thirsty and hot from the hunt, came upon a spring so pure and clear that it seemed liquid silver. No leaf floated upon its untroubled surface; it might have been a mirror for the gods. He dropped to his knees on the grass at its brim and leaned his head down to drink from it. When his thirst was slaked, he raised his head and saw that there was a marvelous boy looking up at him from the water. Strange feelings invaded him. He wanted only to merge himself with this wonderful creature. "Oh, come to me,"

he murmured. He opened his arms and the boy opened his. He lowered his head and offered his lips; the boy in the water seemed to yearn up at him, but could not be touched. "Why are you teasing me?" asked Narcissus. "I know—you are treating me just as I've treated those who love me. But be merciful, let me embrace you!" And he wept with frustration into the little pool, from which his beloved seemed to mock him.

At last something, perhaps it was Nemesis, made him

understand that the wonderful creature he adored was himself. Still he could not break the spell. He thrust his hands into the pool to grasp that splendid head, to caress those vibrant golden curls, but the youth disappeared in the rippling water. "No," called Narcissus, "no, don't leave me. I know you are myself, but I shall die if I can't go on gazing at you forever." And there he lay, at the water's edge, gazing and murmuring, lovingly, despairingly, dying with love for himself. He, too, grew thin and wasted, and though he suffered to see his image dwindling, he could not bear to tear himself away. "Alas," he sighed, "alas." And then, "Ah, youth beloved in vain, farewell!"

And Echo, who still watched over him, repeated, "Alas. Ah, youth beloved in vain, farewell!"

Even when he was crossing the river that lies at the lip of the Land of the Dead, Narcissus leaned over the side of the boat that carried him, for one last look at his own dear face. When the nymphs came to bury his body they found no trace of him, but an exquisite flower had appeared where he died, with snow-white petals and a golden yellow center. They named it narcissus. It springs up at the end of winter and is said to provide a cure for frostbite.

BELLEROPHON

Bellerophon, the reckless son of King Glaucus of Corinth (or perhaps, it was whispered, of Poseidon), killed his brother, Deliades. It was an accident, but he was a hotheaded fellow and had already slain another youth, so he was forced to flee.

He sought sanctuary in Argos, where King Proetus took him in, purified him of his transgression, and treated him with great courtesy. Bellerophon was engaging and comely, and Proetus's wife, Anteia, soon fell desperately in love with him. Perhaps he amused himself by teasing her a little, perhaps she misunderstood. In any event, the queen offered herself to him, but he would have none of her.

"The gods would destroy me," he said disdainfully, "if I were to repay the kindness of my host by dilly-dallying with my hostess."

Mortified by this rejection, she went to her husband. "Your

insufferable guest," she sobbed, "has assaulted me. My honor, and yours, demand that he be killed."

"Weep no more, beloved," Proetus whispered. "This loathsome fellow has eaten at my table and sheltered under my roof. If I were to rase my hand against him, the Furies would wreak vengeance upon me. But be sure of this: The earth will drink his blood."

"Soon," whispered Anteia, "it must be soon." The next morning he called his guest to him and handed him a sealed letter, saying, "You are young and lively, and must be growing restless here, with so little to divert you. Do take this letter for me to Iobates, King of Lycia, who is my wife's father. You will be doing me a greater service than you can imagine, and he will make your life more interesting, I'm sure."

Bellerophon was jubilant at this opportunity to escape the court and to see Asia for the first time. When he arrived in Lycia, King Iobates entertained his charming guest handsomely with feasts and athletic contests for nine days, before he even thought to open his son-in-law's letter. He was aghast at what he read there. "Bellerophon, who brings you this letter, is a brave warrior, an invincible hero, and a vile worm. He has tried to lay his filthy hands upon your daughter. Please destroy him."

Iobates did not care to arouse the rage of the Furies, any more than Proetus had. "Bellerophon, my dear friend," he said to the unsuspecting fellow, "my son-in-law commends you to the skies. He says you are a brave and daring warrior; and bravery and daring are exactly what is needed in Lycia now. Have you heard of the Chimæra? She has a lion's head, the body of a goat, the tail of a serpent, and she breathes fire. She is a dreadful scourge upon my lands, and I would be awfully glad to be rid of her." He did not add that she was unconquerable and would surely put an end to his inconvenient guest.

"Not another word, good Iobates," interrupted Bellerophon. "I am grateful for the chance to repay your hospitality." Indeed he was growing tired of his own exemplary behavior—and he welcomed the chance for a bit of a tussle. He raced off to consult the soothsayer Polyidus on how best to go about it. The seer advised him readily:

> "To overcome the beast you must
> First catch the untamed Pegasus—
> Born from a drop of blood, 'tis said,
> That fell from slain Medusa's head.
> Athene's help is what you need
> To win that marvelous, wingèd steed."

Bellerophon went immediately to Athene's temple and spent the night there. Sure enough, the goddess appeared to him in a dream. She handed him a golden bridle, saying, "You will find your mount at the well of Pirene. If you can saddle him, he will carry you wherever you wish to go." And when Bellerophon awoke, the bridle lay gleaming beside him. He took it, hurried to the well, and found Pegasus drinking there, just as Athene had promised. The huge horse came to him willingly and even bent its head for the bridle.

Bellerophon leaped upon its back, and it carried him to where the Chimæra was rampaging about the countryside, dining on youths and maidens, which she preferred to the old and leathery.

> "Old folks have horrid gristly strips
> that bruise a monster's dainty lips,"

she explained. And as she devoured the youths, she chanted gleefully:

> "A tender maid for breakfast,
> A toothsome lad for lunch,
> Oh, the succulent flesh
> Of the young and the fresh!
> Crunch, crunch, crunch."

Hovering above the hideous creature, Bellerophon shot all his arrows straight into her belly, and when she howled her agony, he stuck a lump of lead onto the point of his spear, and jammed it down between her jaws. The fire of her breath melted the lead, and it poured down her throat and into her belly, and the great beast died.

Bellerophon flew back on Pegasus to report his success to Iobates. The disappointed king praised him extravagantly and lost no time in sending him off on a series of other perilous tasks, but each time he managed to triumph over his adversaries. At last, when Bellerophon returned from his final exploit, he was met by the palace guard, dispatched by the desperate Iobates to eliminate him once and for all. Seeing himself so outnumbered, he dismounted and called out to Poseidon:

"Great Poseidon, pray, attend me—
Send thy waters to defend me!"

And the sea god came to his aid. Poseidon sent a boiling flood at Bellerophon's heels as he strode toward the royal palace. Fearing for their lives, the Lycian women rushed out to meet him. They threw their skirts up to their hips, above

their bellies, uncovering everything, proffering everything, turning themselves about wildly and crying out to him,

> "Welcome, Bellerophon, wonderful hero!
> Gladly we greet you, both front-o and rear-o!
> Do not destroy us—
> Stop and enjoy us!"

Bellerophon, appalled and embarrassed, turned and fled. Poseidon's waves withdrew before him, and Iobates, now convinced of his guest's propriety, ran out after him.

"Stop, stop, Bellerophon," he shouted after the retreating hero, "how can you think of leaving us? I see that you are a virtuous man, and that the gods favor you. Take my daughter, Philonoë, as your wife, and when I die you shall have my kingdom." Then they embraced and returned to the palace, where the evil letter was shown, and Bellerophon told his story.

So Bellerophon and Philonoë were wed, and enjoyed some happiness together. But Bellerophon had developed a taste for risky adventures. In time he became restless and much too ambitious, so that one day he actually took it into his head to fly up to Olympus, thinking himself fit to join the immortals there.

"Look at this!" exclaimed Zeus. "A presumptuous fellow on a steed much too good for him." And he sent a gadfly to sting Pegasus on the rump, just under his tail. The horse reared up and threw Bellerophon back to Earth. Then Pegasus flew on to Olympus, where Zeus received him enthusiastically. He became the pride of Zeus's stable, and was even given the honor of bearing the great god's lightning and thunder.

But Bellerophon did not fare so well. He wandered alone for the rest of his days—blind and lame, shunned by both gods and men.

THESEUS

I've been to Corinth to consult with the sorceress," said King Aegeus. "Medea. Enchanting woman. Attractive woman. Very obliging." Aegeus was enjoying a drink with King Pittheus of Troezen and his daughter, Aethra, on his way home to Athens. "I told her how sorely my heart yearns for a son."

"Ah. No offspring?" asked Pittheus, refilling his guest's glass.

"No, sir. But Medea said to me, 'Well, you shall have one. I'll see to it. All I ask is your protection, in Athens, against my enemies.' 'And what enemies are those?' I asked her. 'Oh,' she said, 'you know how ill-natured people can be.' We parted on excellent terms."

"Drink up, drink up," urged his host, with a squint at Aethra. "I can almost feel the power of Medea here in the wine. Drink up, both of you." And it was not long before he was shooing the two of them, giggling like adolescents, into Aethra's bed-chamber. Pittheus felt sorry for his daughter. She was officially betrothed to the madcap Bellerophon, but he had long since been packed off in disgrace, and the poor girl had languished, a hopeless virgin, until Aegeus that night relieved her of her burdensome maidenhood.

When at length the lovers fell asleep, Athene came to Aethra in a dream. The city of Troezen was dedicated to Athene and Poseidon, so when the goddess ordered Aethra up out of bed and down to the seashore, the weary girl did as she was told. When she arrived at the water's edge, she heard Athene once again, saying, "Lift up your skirt and wade out to Sphaeria. When you reach the island, you will know what to do." But when Aethra reached the island, there was noth-ing she could do, because Poseidon, having conspired with Athene, was there to receive her and to ravish her. Perhaps "ravish" is not quite the appropriate word: there is no reason to assume that this double deflowerment was the least bit dis-tasteful to the former virgin. In fact, she later decreed that each Troezenian maiden must dedicate her girdle to Athene before her marriage.

At any rate, Aethra returned to her bed, where, next morn-ing, she and Aegeus enjoyed one final round of celebration. "I'm off to Athens," he sighed. "But if a son [he said nothing of a daughter] should be born of our pleasure, do not put the boy in a wild place to die, nor send him off to be reared by strangers. Raise him up nicely yourself, but in secret—for I have fifty greedy nephews who presume themselves my heirs, and they are not likely to wish you, or him, well." Then he led her out to the road and found a great rock, under which he buried his sword and spare sandals. He heaved the rock back into place and said, "When the boy has grown strong enough to lift this rock, give him these tokens and send him to me in Athens. Take care of yourself, my dear," he added, and set off for home.

In due time, a son was born, and Poseidon magnanimously allowed Aegeus the credit. Aethra and Pittheus raised the child till he was sixteen, a strong—and headstrong—youth. When she saw that he was ready, Aethra led him to the rock and asked him to lift it. He laughed, rolled it away as if it were an apple, and took up the sword and sandals that lay beneath it.

"Now, my child," said his mother sadly, "it is time for you to go to Athens and claim your place." Then she told him the story of his conception—and hinted that Poseidon might also be considered his father. Theseus was on fire to leave at once. His grandfather offered him a fine ship for his journey, and his mother begged him to accept it.

"I won't be packed off safely to my father, like a child," said

Theseus; "that's not my idea of making my way in the world. I'll go on foot, *because* it is so hazardous. I mean to be as great a hero as my cousin Hercules." And though his mother wept and his grandfather sighed, he set off on the dangerous coastal road to Athens, with Aegeus's old sandals on his feet, the sword at his hip, and a glint in his eye.

The country was overrun with villains, robbers, rogues, knaves, and rascals of every kind, and Theseus was resolved to do what Hercules would have done—rid the world of them all. In the spirit of fairness, and to make the game more interesting, he decided to dispatch the villains with their own weapons. By nightfall of the first day he had already taken his first trophy, the iron club of a vicious son of Vulcan, who died under the same weapon with which he had killed countless travelers.

His next encounter was with the dreaded Sinis, a savage creature of great strength who specialized in bending the tops of two pine trees till they brushed the earth, tying the arms of a traveler to them, and letting go, so that his victim was untidily bisected. Theseus served Sinis as the brute had served others, and continued on his way till he reached the high, rocky cliffs where the notorious bandit Sciron made his camp. It was Sciron's pleasure to force passersby to kneel before him and wash his feet. When they had done as he ordered, he would roar delightedly:

"You've cleaned the dirt between my toes,
You're cross, the sweat runs down your nose,
Think how refreshing it would be
To take a swim. Farewell! You're free!"

And with one mighty kick he would send his victim over the cliff and into the sea, where a giant turtle lay impatiently waiting for his dinner. Theseus readily dispatched Sciron by the same route. The turtle feasted on the monster, and may be waiting yet for his next meal.

Theseus battled so many and slew them so appropriately that he became renowned throughout Greece. His most famous conquest was the depraved Procrustes the Stretcher, who had an iron bed upon which he laid his victims. Those who were too long to fit it were trimmed to the proper length; those who were too short were stretched. Theseus, having administered the necessary alterations, left Procrustes to die upon his own bed.

Theseus did as he had promised to do—he killed every one of the brigands who had terrorized the notorious coastal road, and when he reached Athens, his name had preceded him. He was welcomed with great honor by King Aegeus, who could not know the hero he embraced was his own son.

Medea knew. A great deal had happened since Aegeus had

come to Corinth to hear her prophecy. Her husband, Jason, had abandoned her, and when she learned that he meant to marry the King of Corinth's daughter, her fury had consumed her. She must have her revenge. As a supposed peace offering, Medea had sent the bride-to-be a golden crown and a long white robe; and when the girl put them on, she burst into flames. Though she jumped into the palace fountain, she was burnt to death, and so were Medea's unfortunate children, King Creon, and almost everyone else in the palace as well. It was then that Medea leaped into her famous chariot drawn by winged serpents, and fled to Athens, demanding sanctuary. King Aegeus did better than that. He married her.

Her sorcery told her that Theseus was the son she had helped Aegeus to sire. But Medea, too, had borne the king a son, and she feared that when he learned this valorous youth was the child of his night with Aethra, he would name the older boy his heir. "The fellow is dangerous," she whispered to her husband. "Your people idolize him, and he is much too full of himself. I am certain he is plotting to overthrow your highness, slay us both, and take your place on the throne."

Aegeus, whose respect for his wife was enormous, agreed to offer the visitor a cup of wine which Medea had spiked with deadly wolfsbane.

Thesus, unsuspecting, stepped forward, took the cup, and

raised it. At that moment, Aegeus saw the sword that Theseus wore, with serpents carved upon its ivory hilt. "My son!" he exclaimed, and knocked the cup from the boy's hand just before it reached his lips. Medea, discovered, wrapped herself and her child in a magic cloud and fled in the chariot once more, this time to Asia.

King Aegeus did proclaim Theseus his son and heir, and all of Athens celebrated vigorously with sacrifices, bonfires, and feasts. The Athenians were overjoyed to claim the glorious young hero their own and hoped, moreover, that he would liberate them from the misery that afflicted them.

It was a lot to expect. The Cretan king, Minos of Cnossus, held Aegeus responsible for the death of his only son, Androgeus, who, while visiting Athens, had attempted to kill a ferocious white bull and was himself killed. For his loss, Minos exacted a grievous price: Every nine years the people of Athens must send him seven maidens and seven youths to be given to the monster, Minotaur, who would devour them. Not long after Theseus had taken his place in the royal court, the terrible tribute was due. Though the victims were traditionally chosen by lot, Theseus insisted upon being among them. He also recruited two brave and clever boys who acted and dressed like girls, and secretly substituted them for two of the maidens.

Aegeus, having found his son, was not at all eager to lose

him, but Theseus laughed at his fears. "Father," he said, "how can you doubt that I will be able to slay one lonely monster? Please tell no one what I'm up to, but give me a white sail as well as a black one, and when you see the white sail coming home, be sure to prepare me a splendid victory feast!"

So the ship departed under its sad black sail. When it reached Crete, the young victims were led through the city streets before the pitying eyes of the population. King Minos himself watched them with a half-smile, but his daughter, Ariadne, lost her heart to the dashing Theseus the minute she saw him. She managed to contrive a secret meeting with him. "The Minotaur is my half-brother," she said. "If you will marry me, I will tell you how to find him in his labyrinth and kill him."

"You shall be my wife," Theseus promised her, "and I will bring you back with me to Athens." Ariadne had a ball of thread that had been given to her by Daedalus. She entrusted it to Theseus, and a magic sword as well. "Wait for me, beloved," said Theseus, and led his trembling young companions into the intricate maze. He tied one end of the thread to the door lintel and let it out at each turn of the way as they walked into the darkness. Theseus went unerringly to the place where the Minotaur lay sleeping, and seizing the hideous creature by its hair, he slew it. Then, rewinding the ball of thread as he went,

he retraced his steps. The boys who were dressed as girls made short work of the guards, and Ariadne ran with the blood-spattered Theseus and his charges to the harbor, where they boarded the black-sailed ship and sailed at once for Athens.

On the way, the voyagers put in at the island of Naxos. Here the story grows dark. While Ariadne lay sleeping on the shore, Theseus and his crew set sail and abandoned her there. Ariadne, awakening, found herself deserted, and called upon the gods for comfort. Her prayers were answered by Dionysus, who came to her rescue and married her without delay. That is one story. There are many others, all trying to make sense of Theseus's ungrateful behavior and Ariadne's fate; no one knows which is true.

When the triumphant ship reached the coast of Attica, Theseus, in his joy to be home, forgot to change the black sail to the white one. His father, who had been keeping a long, weary watch for his son's return, called out, "It is the black sail, it is the sail of death!" And he leaped into the sea from the Acropolis where he stood and drowned. The Aegean Sea is named in his memory.

So Theseus became the ruler of Athens, and he fashioned a state both wise and just, governed by its citizens, a sanctuary for all who needed one. It was Theseus who welcomed the outcast Oedipus; and Theseus who sheltered his great cousin, Hercules, when the rest of the world shunned him, horrified by the monstrous crimes he had committed in his madness.

Theseus's restless spirit never forsook him. He sailed off many times in pursuit of adventure and played a valorous part in many wars. Somehow he managed to find time for countless romantic escapades as well. He decided, when Helen—later of Troy—was a little girl, that he would marry her when she grew up; and with the help of his friend, Pirithous, he kidnapped her.

He didn't hold her for long. Her brothers, Castor and Pollux, raided the town where he had left her, and brought her home with them.

Undaunted, Theseus went to Amazonia and abducted the Queen of the Amazons, Hippolyte. When her fierce tribe of women warriors came to Attica to fetch her back, there was a bloody battle. The Amazons were repulsed, and Hippolyte was left behind.

When Pirithous, in his turn, took a notion to kidnap Persephone from Hades, bring her back to the upper world, and marry her, Theseus did not hesitate to descend to Tartarus with him, straight down to the great hall where Hades and Persephone sat on their twin thrones. But Hades understood very well why the two men had honored him with a visit. "My dear friends," he said, "welcome. Make yourselves comfortable. You must certainly stay a while with me." And offered them chairs. As soon as they were seated, Theseus and Pirithous forgot why they had come, for these were the Chairs of Forgetfulness. "My house is your house," said Hades with a grin.

And indeed they remained thus imprisoned for four years, guarded by serpents and tormented by the Furies. Their flesh melted into their seats; they could not tear themselves away. At last Hercules arrived in the Land of the Dead on an errand of his own and managed to wrench Theseus from his chair and carry him back to the upper world. Unfortunately, a good bit of his posterior was left behind, and that, it is said, is why Athenians who are descended from him have such small backsides. Hades kept hold of the ill-fated Pirithous, whose suffering went on unabated, because he had had the temerity to covet Queen Persephone.

Theseus's good luck did not last forever. He murdered Hippolyte (in circumstances that reflected badly on him), but not before she had borne him a son, Hippolytus. This child grew up to be an exceedingly handsome young man, and Theseus loved him dearly. He was as brave and charming as his father, but there was this difference between them—Hippolytus wanted nothing whatever to do with women; he could not abide their company. He worshiped at the shrine of the chaste huntress, Artemis, which offended Aphrodite.

> "He who scorns love's goddess must
> Fall victim to a woman's lust!"

she decreed, and by way of revenge, she maliciously caused Theseus's young wife, Phaedra, Ariadne's sister, to fall in love with Hippolytus.

The bewitched woman wrestled with her forbidden passion, but she could not overcome what the goddess had forced upon her. At last, gaunt and wretched, she gave in to it, and wrote a letter to Hippolytus, offering to become his mistress. Hippolytus was outraged. He burned the letter as if he feared to be contaminated by it, and stormed into Phaedra's chamber, shouting, "All women are loathsome, and you are the foulest of them all, with your vile suggestions. Do you dare ask me to betray my father with his own wife?"

Phaedra, fearing to be found out by her husband, tore off her clothes and screamed at the top of her lungs, "Help me, save me, he is attacking me!" Hippolytus backed away from the wild woman in terror and ran away. Phaedra, in despair and humiliation, hanged herself, but not before she left a letter to her husband, accusing Hippolytus of an assortment of vicious crimes.

The bereaved Theseus believed his wife's accusations. "Poseidon, my father," he begged, "I call down your curse upon this cur who has defiled my wife!" And then he banished the boy, saying, "Go, you are an exile and a stranger to me, and I lay my curse and my father's curse upon you!"

Father Poseidon was listening. Hippolytus, mortally wounded by his father's rejection, ran to his chariot, and flew off in it, hardly knowing what he did. As he careened around a curve, his horses were startled by a monster that arose suddenly from the waves beside the road, and Hippolytus was thrown from the chariot and killed. Then Artemis came to Theseus, saying, "Be comforted. The letter was false. This was all the doing of spiteful Aphrodite. Both your wife and your son came under her evil spell." When Theseus learned that his son had been falsely accused, he was lacerated with remorse and sorrow. Nothing could comfort him: His wife and son were lost.

But by and by he took up his old adventurous ways again, and the Athenians grew impatient with his many love affairs and lost their liking for him. So Theseus was forced to leave home, an exile, and take shelter with his friend, King Lycomedes, on Scyros, where Theseus owned property. His host greeted him with great ceremony. A bull was sacrificed, and a fine feast was given. Wine was consumed in vast quantities. "Come, noble Theseus," said the king, "what better time than this for us to walk the boundaries of your estate together? That land is so fair that I have often coveted it for myself." He couldn't have been more honest than that. Arm in arm the two men walked together, admiring the lemon trees, the olive groves, and the fine views. "From this high cliff," said Lycomedes, "you will be able to see it all." And when they had reached the summit, he clapped Theseus hard on the shoulder and sent him over the edge to his death. "What a pity," he sighed afterwards. "The poor man had drunk so much he couldn't see properly and stepped right over the edge, with a smile on his face."

That was not quite the last of Theseus. His spirit is said to have risen from the earth to lead the Greeks to victory over the Persians; and the Delphic Oracle commanded the Athenians to bring his body home. In time Theseus's bones were returned from exile to Athens and placed in a temple, the Theseum, which became a sanctuary for fugitives, in his honor.

ORPHEUS AND EURYDICE

When Orpheus played his lyre and sang, even the gods stopped their intriguing and philandering and listened like children. Men and women froze in their tracks, then dropped everything to run after him; trees danced for him, their limbs waving, their leaves fluttering. Rocks melted, rivers twisted like eels in their beds to come to him, and the wild beasts lay at his feet, beating time with their paws.

It was Orpheus's music that saved the Argonauts when they let their ship stray from its course to listen to the Sirens, those monsters who began at the top as women, and finished with the tail-feathers of birds. Their song was so seductive that poor sailors who heard it were lost in it, forgot their homes, their wives, their very bodies, so that they starved themselves to death while drinking in the Sirens' fatal song. Orpheus played and sang for the Argonauts, drowning out the fatal music with his own, while they regained their course. He was irresistible, and no wonder—his mother, Calliope, chief of the Muses, taught him to sing, and Apollo, that incomparable musician, gave him his lyre.

Every girl came under his spell; and when he fell deeply in love with the dryad Eurydice, he had no trouble winning her heart.

"Will you not come to me,
Blessèd Eurydice?"

was all it took to enchant her. Orpheus planned a magnificent wedding feast, and invited Hymen, god of nuptials, to attend them. The god came from Crete in his saffron robe to celebrate their marriage and to bring good fortune, but the wedding day was marred by bad omens. The torch that Hymen brought to light their way refused to burn; it smoldered and smoked and made the guests' eyes smart, so that they shed unlucky tears and shook their heads with foreboding.

They did not have long to wait for the fulfillment of these evil signs. While the men were drinking yet another bawdy toast to the groom, the bride and her nymphs covered their ears and ran laughing together across the lawn. Eurydice, dancing

her happiness, kicked up her heels and disturbed a serpent in the grass. It lifted its head and bit her on the ankle; in an instant she was dead.

They brought her lifeless body to Orpheus, and he was beyond reason. He ran this way and that, pounding his breast, howling his anguish to every creature on earth, beseeching the gods for compassion. Bur Eurydice was gone; she had entered the Land of the Dead. Then Orpheus seized his lyre and rushed down into the Underworld, playing and singing so passionately of his lost love that the ferryman, Charon, took pity on him and let him cross, and Cerberus, the snake-haired guardian dog of Hades, only whined a little as he entered the utter darkness of Tartarus.

When at last Orpheus stood before the thrones of Hades and Persephone, his fingers trembled on the lyre, and his voice was as liquid as his tears.

> "You gods of darkness, to whom all men come,
> Wicked or just, defiant, craven, dumb,
> Each in his proper hour, to stand, aghast,
> For judgment, when his earthly time has passed,
> Give back Eurydice—so new, so fresh—
> Her little feet so light they'd scarcely left
> Their imprint on the earth. I pray you, lend
> Me what was mine. She will be yours again.
> Return my tender girl, who has but strayed
> From life. I swear the debt will be repaid.
> Or keep us both, and gain a double death.
> Without her, I'll forsake both song and breath."

The ghosts of the dead forgot their own agonies and suffered with him. The Furies, those inexorable avengers of evil, wept. Tears of blood ran down their stony cheeks. Persephone, turning to Hades, sighed, and even that cruel ruler of the dead was moved by Orpheus's extremity. He nodded, and Eurydice came, limping slightly from the serpent's fang, dazed from her recent draught of Lethe, half-knowing her husband, already half-forgetful of her life.

"Take her," said Hades, "but hear this one condition: You may lead her to the upper earth; she will be yours. But if you look back even once before the sun's rays fall on both your heads, one single glance, then she is lost to you forever."

So Orpheus, not daring to show his joy, led his beloved solemnly through the dead-silent, midnight halls; he guided her feet with his lyre and his song along the steep and rocky path, until at last he stepped out onto a grassy field, into the sunlight. He turned, then, his arms outstretched to embrace her, but she had not yet made the final step; her head was still shrouded in darkness. So quickly, her arms that strained toward his wavered and vanished; her voice calling "Farewell! Farewell!" was more imagined than heard. He was alone.

Orpheus, in an agony of guilt and loss, raced after her, skidded and stumbled down the stony path to the Underworld, and begged Charon to ferry him again to the Land of the Dead,

so he might try once more to ransom back his love. But stony
Charon turned his head away.

For seven days Orpheus fasted by the river, cursing the cruel
gods, cursing his life. At last he rose, went up into the land of

the living, and wandered about the Thracian countryside, singing of his loss so mournfully that all of nature grieved with him.

Three years he lived in this way. He refused any comfort; he refused the many women who yearned to help him forget his lost Eurydice. Then he declared that henceforth the love of young boys would be his only consolation. That, and of course his lyre, which he played almost without ceasing, but only the one sorrowful song.

Eventually he turned to the worship of Apollo and became a priest in his temple. One day a group of Maenads burst into the temple, drunk and frenzied by their celebration of Bacchus and enraged at Orpheus for having spurned them. They slew their husbands, who were worshipping there, then murdered Orpheus and tore him limb from limb. His head and his lyre they flung into the river Hebrus, which carried them, still singing woefully, to the island of Lesbos, where the tearful Muses buried them. Then they gathered up his limbs, and those they buried too, at the foot of Mount Olympus. And there the nightingales sing, to this day, more sweetly than they do in any other place.

THE GODS

APHRODITE—goddess of love and beauty

APOLLO—son of Zeus; god of light and truth; greatest musician, archer, healer

ARTEMIS—twin sister to Apollo; goddess of the hunt

ATHENE—Daughter of Zeus; goddess of wisdom, war, and the useful arts; she sprang, full-grown, from his brow

DEMETER—sister of Zeus; supreme earth goddess

DIANA—Roman name for Artemis

HADES—brother of Zeus; lord of the Underworld

HECATE—goddess of witches, darkness, the dead

HEPHAESTUS—son of Hera, god of fire, metalsmith of the gods

HERA—wife of Zeus, also his sister

HERMES—son of Zeus, and his messenger; the shrewdest of the gods, and also the guide of the dead

JUNO—Roman name for Hera

JUPITER—Roman name for Zeus

KORE—Demeter's daughter, later known as Persephone

MERCURY—Roman name for Hermes

MINERVA—Roman name for Athene

NEPTUNE—Roman name for Poseidon

PAN—son of Hermes, and part man, part goat; a lesser earth god, famous for his pipe playing and his lusty nature

PERSEPHONE—also known as Kore, daughter of Demeter; goddess of Spring and Queen of the Underworld

POSEIDON—brother of Zeus; lord of the sea

PROTEUS—Wisest of the sea gods, he can foretell the future and change his shape at will.

RHEA—mother of Zeus, Hades, and Demeter

SILENUS—son of Hermes, associated with Pan; a drunkard

TRITON—son of Poseidon, trumpeter of the sea

VENUS—Roman name for Aphrodite

ZEUS—Supreme deity, ruler of the gods

The Old Testament
Made Easy

For Melinda, Sidonie, Jonas, and Emma

And God Said, "Let Us Make Man"

"All this in just six days!" God cried.
"I am supremely satisfied.
Those dainty finned and creeping things,
The ones with hooves, the ones with wings!
This world's divine. Just one thing more—
Two-legged, furless omnivore.
Free will, at least to some degree.
The creature quite resembles me.
It only wants a breath of life;
And then, of course, it wants a wife.
No sooner asked, my boy, than done!
They will afford me hours of fun.
See how they blink, and stretch, and grin.
Now let the comedy begin!"

In the Garden

"My darling Rib," said Adam, "please—
It isn't any use to tease.
I don't want fruit. I've just had lunch."
"One bite!" begged Eve. "You'll love the crunch!"

The Invention of Murder

Cain, in a brutish frenzy, rose
And struck his brother dead.
The Lord was moved to fulminate
Upon his wretched head.

"Am I my brother's keeper, then?"
Cain peevishly inquired.
"You are," said God, "and you have caused
That brother to expire.

"I set my mark upon your brow.
You'll find no place to hide.
Go forth, abhorred by every man,
O filthy fratricide!"

So Cain went out to dwell in Nod,
He wedded and begat.
And Adam sired another son.
"Well, that," said God, "is that."

Methuselah

Insufficiently funded with facts,
We can cite only two of his acts:
Begat Lamech, age one eighty-seven;
Age nine sixty-nine, went to heaven.

A Hard Voyage

Said God, "This contemptible race
Has proved itself shockingly base.
Such rascals! Confound them,
I fear I must drown them.
They're sinning all over the place.

"You, Noah, deserve to be saved,
For you're not even mildly depraved.
Build an ark. Make it huge,
To withstand the deluge,
Lest you sink to a watery grave."

Then Noah (his family, too)
Assembled an unabridged zoo.
"What a stench!" Noah cried,
Hanging over the side.
"Every one of them needs a shampoo."

Forty days, forty nights, how it poured!
They were itchy, rheumatic, and bored.
But they weathered the flood,
And debarked in the mud.
"Last one off is a slug!" said the Lord.

The Tower of Babel

The descendants of Noah
(Which no one was not)
All spoke the same language,
All dwelt in one spot.

They were building a tower,
It reached to the sky.
"I call *this*," said Jehovah,
"Egregiously high.

"They are inches from heaven.
The next thing you know,
They'll be right in our laps.
That tower must go!

"One has got to deal firmly
With people like these,
For they're apt to forget
Why I gave them their knees.

"I shall send them all packing—
They'll learn to obey!
Let their tongues be bamboozled!
Let babble hold sway!"

And that's why new languages,
Rich and complex,
Were invented by Frenchmen
And Urdus and Czechs.

An Unfortunate Incident

"Cursèd Sodom," God raged, "is an outpost of hell!
I consign it to flames—and Gomorrah as well."

Two angels, dispatched for the purpose, told Lot:
"Clear out of here fast, before things get too hot.
This cesspool called Sodom is doomed. You're excused—
Just don't ever look back. God would not be amused."

In a shower of brimstone and fire, Lot fled,
But his wife absentmindedly swiveled her head.
She was changed to a pillar of salt, Mrs. Lot.
I, for one, don't believe she deserved what she got.

Disaster Narrowly Averted

When Sarah, nearly ninety-one,
Bore Abraham an infant son,
They conscientiously revised him—
That is to say, they circumcised him—
According to the will of God,
Who doesn't like to spare the rod.

They doted fiercely on the child,
A fault that drove the Good Lord wild.
"Go, Abraham, and render me
Your dear son's life," commanded He.
"Your ardor has been misdirected.
Young Isaac must be vivisected."

"My Lord," groaned Abraham, "he's Thine!"
His ancient eyes filled up with brine;
And though the fearful edict crushed him,
He took the boy and neatly trussed him
And settled him upon a pyre.
He raised his knife. He raised it higher . . .

"Stay!" cried an angel. "Abraham!
God sends a sacrificial ram.
Cut Isaac loose, the trial is ended.
Your piety's to be commended."
Wept Abraham, "The Lord is good."
One hopes that Isaac understood.

Twins

Esau said, "I'm feeling faint."

"Aw," said Jacob, "no, you ain't."

"Papa's blessing," Esau cried,

"Is mine by rights. But I'll have died

Of hunger first. For pity's sake—

My birthright for your lentils, Jake."

"Your birthright?" Jacob murmured. "Sold!

Dig in, before the stuff gets cold."

Jacob's Ladder

Mused Jacob: "A singular dream!
That ladder! Those angels agleam!
And the Lord blessed my seed—
Which is just what I need.
What a boost for the old self-esteem!"

A Romance

Jacob fancied Cousin Rachel,
Uncle Laban's comely child.
Seven years he toiled to earn her,
While her glances drove him wild.

When at last his bride was bedded,
Jacob drew the veil to kiss her.
Under it was Cousin Leah,
Rachel's older, squint-eyed sister.

"Be not so distraught," said Laban.
"Though at first she looks alarming,
Leah's fun. I'll throw in Rachel—
All for seven years of farming!

"Only seven more, dear nephew,
For the pair. You find that shocking?
Rachel will divert you nicely,
Leah darns a dandy stocking.

"Take the two. And take their handmaids—
This, I think, is rather lavish—
Saucy Bilhah, nubile Zilpah.
Both of them are yours to ravish!"

Leah bore him seven children,
Zilpah had a couple more.
Rachel and her handmaid, Bilhah,
Managed yet another four.

One of Leah's was a daughter.
Sons made up the other dozen.
All twelve tribes of Israel sprang from
Jacob's craving for his cousin.

The Story of Joseph (Mercifully Condensed)

"Come see my pretty coat," said Joseph.
"Papa gave me it."
"What horrid taste!" his brothers cried,
And threw him in a pit.

They hauled him out and sold him to
A band of traveling men,
Who headed south for Egypt, where
They sold him off again.

But Joseph landed on his feet.
He found he had a bent
For listening to Pharaoh's dreams
And telling what they meant.

When, by and by, the folks back home
Turned up in Egypt's land,
How goggle-eyed they were to find
Their Joseph in command.

He greeted them affectingly,
And made a joyful noise,
Exclaiming, "Oh, my dear Papa!"
And "No hard feelings, boys.

"Come, Hebrews all, and pitch your tents
Beside the glittering Nile.
For I am Pharaoh's fair-haired boy!"
Said they, "The kid's got style."

Dispensation

Unless you like stats,
Just skip the begats.

On the Banks of the Nile

The daughter of Pharaoh
Was thrilled to the marrow
When Moses turned up.
(He was cute as a pup.)

Crying, "Isn't he luscious!"
She snatched from the rushes
The child of the Jews,
Who would later make news.

Captivity

"Tell Pharaoh Jehovah proposes,"
Said God, "that the Hebrews go free."
"You know, I st-stutter," said Moses.
"He'll never l-listen to me."

Said Pharaoh, "It's out of the question.
I won't be deprived of my Jews."
Said Moses, "J-just a suggestion.
But I'm glad I'm n-not in your shoes."

"L-Lord," Moses groaned, "it looks hopeless.
He won't l-let loose of us Jews."
Said God, "Then I'll plague him with locusts.
The wretch is absurdly obtuse."

164

The Ten Commandments

"With the tip of my terrible finger I write
My laws on a couple of stones.
You, Moses, make sure you hold on to them tight,"
Said the Lord in implacable tones.

"They're heavy," groaned Moses. "And what if I fall?
I'll break *all* Ten Commandments at once.
No offense, but I wish you had written them small—
I'm g-getting too old for such stunts."

Heroism

The Canaanites, for twenty years,
Had punctured hapless Jews with spears.
The Israelites at last uprose
And slew their Canaanitish foes.
Bad Captain Sisera alone
Survived and, eager to postpone—
Or better yet, prevent—his end,
Sought sanctuary with a friend.
Who wasn't in. His wife, Jael,
Cooed, "Captain, you're not looking well.
My tent is yours. May I suggest
A nap? Stretch out, take off your vest,
Perhaps you'd like a glass of milk?"
Her voice was soft as spider silk.
(Four lines that follow may offend.
If squeamish, skip and read the end.)
The villain slept. She tiptoed round
And nailed his noggin to the ground.
To guarantee that he was dead,
She severed the unsightly head.
"All hail, Jael!" the Hebrews sang.
"That varmint was too mean to hang!"

Gossip

"There goes that lunatic, Samson,
Running off to his trollop, Delilah.
The fellow just can't keep his pants on.
Have you ever seen anything viler?"

Luck

Ibical-bibical,
Boaz of Bethlehem,
Single, respectable,
Very well-heeled,

Caught the attention of
Young widow Ruth, who was
Complementarily
Poor. But genteel.

Divine Retribution

When the Hebrews and Philistines fought to the death,
The idolatrous Philistine horde
Slew a great many Jews and, though quite out of breath,
Made off with the Ark of the Lord.

And His vengeance was swift, and His vengeance was hot.
"Alas!" they exclaimed. "How it smarts!"
For He smote them with hemorrhoids. Cruel, was it not?
They had rather been smitten with warts.

Epitaph

Here lieth
Goliath.

Nothing stopped him
Till David dropped him.

A Tribute

Of worthy Samuel I sing,
Who never (what a shame!) was King.
His task it was to find, appoint,
And with a drop of oil anoint
The Kings of Israel. He first
Selected Saul, a man accurst.
Undaunted, he chose David next—
Brave, charismatic, oversexed.
As far as anyone could tell,
The only flaw in Samuel
Was this: a tendency to shout
And flap his skinny arms about.

Bad News

Despondent and given to fits,
King Saul, at the end of his wits,
Was informed by a ghost
That the Philistine host
Would chop him, next day, into bits.

A Scandal

Uriah the Hittite's wife, Bathsheba,
Was as dumb and curvaceous as an amoeba.
Which is what prompted King Dave
To misbehave.

Justice Is Served

Pigheaded, wicked Absalom!
He tried to steal his father's throne.
(His father was King David, who
Had recently been wicked, too.)

Insolent Absalom! The fool
Rode off to battle on a mule.
He caught his head upon a limb;
The mule strolled out from under him.

Poor, hapless Absalom! In vain
His roaring, kicking, raising Cain.
He dangled, helpless, by his chin
Till someone came and did him in.

The revolution having failed,
One would expect that peace prevailed.
But David bellowed, overcome,
"Oh, how I miss my Absalom!"

Solomon Sings

True, my marriages *are* frequent
(As some people have complained).
I find foreign girls so piquant,
My miscegenary passions can't be reined.
                    Can not be reined!

Now, Egyptian girls are moody,
And Moabites are bold.
Jewish girls are goody-goody,
With a suffocating tendency to scold.
                    Oh, how they scold!

There's no doubt my lust's excessive
(Seven hundred foreign wives!),
But my stamina's impressive—
I've three hundred foreign concubines besides.
                    I said besides!

Time, I'm certain, will be gracious
When it tallies up my wrongs.
How, if I were less salacious,
Could I write my magnum opus, *Song of Songs*?
                    That *Song of Songs*!

A Bad End

Jezebel, King Ethbaal's daughter,
Practiced witchcraft, crimped her hair,
Worshipped Baal, wore too much makeup,
Drove Elijah to despair.

Sordid creature! Dogs devoured her,
Though the brutes, it seems, had qualms.
Several parts they couldn't stomach—
Skull, and perfumed feet, and palms.

Notes on the Prophet Elijah

Nobody cared to incite
Elijah, the hairy Tishbite.
When he called for a drought, it got dry.
When he called for a death, it was definitely good-bye.

He was fed by ravens.
He was fed by a widow.
He was fed by an angel.
Whenever he wanted to eat,
God sent meat.

Nobody crossed that prophet,
Though they yearned to yell, "STOP IT!"
He called down fire out of heaven and burnt up fifty-one men.
Twice.
So nobody ever said, "Elijah's a tough son of a bitch but
basically nice."

The Esther Story

High-handed Haman, esteemed by the King,
Did an evil, ignoble—nay, damnable—thing.
He proclaimed, "We have too many Hebrews by far.
Let them therefore be slain, in the month of Adar."
When the news reached Queen Esther, she shivered a bit,
Then cried: "Down, I say, *down* with this scrofulous writ!"

She invited her husband and Haman to feast.
When they'd guzzled their fill, and their chins were well greased,
Said King Ahasuerus, "Dear Lady, bravo!
What gift shall I give you, what trinket bestow?
What prize will you claim for those tasty ragouts?"
Said she, "Save my life! And my people—the Jews."

"Who threatens my Queen? What despicable hound?"
Esther pointed to Haman, who fell to the ground.
King Ahasuerus was horribly wroth.
His eyes were afire, his lips were afroth.
Very little remains of this story to tell.
Horrid Haman was hanged, and his ten sons as well.

The festival Purim, which Hebrews observe,
Commemorates Esther—her cunning, her verve.
They dress up in costumes, and sing jolly tunes,
And eat hamantaschen, a cookie with prunes.

Realism

Is the Book of Job
An attempt to probe
The question of why God made a wager with Satan at Job's expense?
Or is it meant to instruct us that, from a celestial point of view,
Whatever we do—or don't do—
The distance between God's understanding and ours is immense?
(Which is why Divine Justice doesn't always make sense.)

In either case, isn't it wise,
Given the vanity of mortal surmise
(Unless, perhaps, you are tempted by Job's dunghill?),
To do nothing so virtuous or so vile
That it prevents you from keeping a low profile?
Attract attention, you're going to foot the bill.
If Satan don't get you, the odds are God will.

189

Jonah

Jonah, the Prophet, reluctant to prophesy,
Fled from Jehovah and hid on a barque.
Found and flung overboard! Swallowed, spat up again!
Syria welcomed him well before dark.

Jonah, much chastened, made haste to prognosticate,
Fresh from the terrible lips of the whale:
"Forty days only till God destroys Nineveh!"
Causing the Ninevan public to quail.

Turning from sin, they repented repeatedly,
Praying and fasting and rolling in mire.
God spared the city and pardoned the populace.
Jonah was cross, for he looked like a liar.

Minor Prophets

The prophets Habakkuk and Amos
Are considerably less famous
Than Isaiah or Jeremiah.
It's not that they lack fire
(The curse of any minor prophet
Can send a miscreant to Tophet).
But when they exhort,
They do keep it short.

Continuity

Our forebears (thanks to good King James)
Talked funny. They had oddish names.
They fell in love, succumbed to lust,
And trampled strangers in the dust.
They suffered flood and fire and drought.
A few of them remained devout.
Their lives were jolly, vapid, grim,
According to Jehovah's whim.
How little things have changed since then!
Whose fault that is, God knows.
                    Amen.